What Was He Doing In Bed With Her?

Even more important, why had she allowed him into her bed?

He'd decided after the night they'd met that he'd be much better off not to call her. His strong reaction to her that night was warning enough. By the next day he'd known that if he continued to see her, they would end up in bed together. He'd reminded himself that Lindsey Russell was not the kind of woman who would be willing to have a no-strings-attached relationship, which was the only kind he was interested in having these days.

Until last night, from the evidence. There were all kinds of strings attached to this scenario, none of them to his liking.

If there was one thing that Jared knew on this particular morning, it was that he had no business being in Lindsey Russell's bed.

What had he been thinking?

Dear Reader,

Welcome to another passionate month at Silhouette Desire where the menu is set with another fabulous title in our DYNASTIES: THE DANFORTHS series. Linda Conrad provides *The Laws of Passion* when Danforth heir Marc must clear his name or face the consequences. And here's a little something to whet your appetite—the second installment of Annette Broadrick's THE CRENSHAWS OF TEXAS. What's a man to do when he's *Caught in the Crossfire*—actually, when he's caught in bed with a senator's daughter? You'll have to wait and see....

Our mouthwatering MANTALK promotion continues with Maureen Child's *Lost in Sensation*. This story, entirely from the hero's point of view, will give you insight into a delectable male—what fun! Kristi Gold dishes up a tasty tidbit with *Daring the Dynamic Sheikh*, the concluding title in her series THE ROYAL WAGER. Rochelle Alers's series THE BLACKSTONES OF VIRGINIA is back with *Very Private Duty* and a hunk you can dig right into. And be sure to save room for the delightful treat that is Julie Hogan's *Business or Pleasure?*

Here's hoping that this month's Silhouette Desire selections will fulfill your craving for the best in sensual romance... and leave you hungry for more!

Happy devouring!

Melissa Jeglinski

Melissa Jeglinski
Senior Editor
Silhouette Desire

ANNETTE BROADRICK

CAUGHT IN THE CROSSFIRE

Published by Silhouette Books
America's Publisher of Contemporary Romance

SILHOUETTE BOOKS

ISBN 0-373-76610-6

CAUGHT IN THE CROSSFIRE

This edition published by arrangement with Harlequin Books S.A.

Visit Silhouette Books at www.eHarlequin.com

Printed in U.S.A.

Books by Annette Broadrick

Silhouette Desire

Hunter's Prey #185
Bachelor Father #219
Hawk's Flight #242
Deceptions #272
Choices #283
Heat of the Night #314
Made in Heaven #336
Return to Yesterday #360
Adam's Story #367
Momentary Marriage #414
With All My Heart #433
A Touch of Spring #464
Irresistible #499
A Loving Spirit #552
Candlelight for Two #577
Lone Wolf #666
Where There Is Love #714
**Love Texas Style!* #734
**Courtship Texas Style!* #739
**Marriage Texas Style!* #745
Zeke #793
**Temptation Texas Style!* #883
Mysterious Mountain Man #925
†*Megan's Marriage* #979
†*The Groom, I Presume?* #992
Lean, Mean & Lonesome #1237
Tall, Dark & Texan #1261
Marriage Prey #1327
◊*Branded* #1604
◊*Caught in the Crossfire* #1610

Silhouette Special Edition

Mystery Wife #877
The President's Daughter #1226
But Not for Me #1472
††*Man in the Mist* #1576
††*Too Tough To Tame* #1581
††*MacGowan Meets His Match* #1586

Silhouette Romance

Circumstantial Evidence #329
Provocative Peril #359
Sound of Summer #412
Unheavenly Angel #442
Strange Enchantment #501
Mystery Lover #533
That's What Friends Are For #544
Come Be My Love #609
A Love Remembered #676
Married?! #742
The Gemini Man #796
Daddy's Angel #976
Impromptu Bride #1018
†*Instant Mommy* #1139
†*Unforgettable Bride* #1294

Silhouette Books

Silhouette Christmas Stories
"Christmas Magic"

Spring Fancy
"Surprise, Surprise!"

Summer Sizzlers
"Deep Cover"

Wanted: Mother
"What's a Dad To Do?"

**Sons of Texas: Rogues and Ranchers*

Do You Take This Man?
"Rent-a-Husband"

**Callaway Country*

Matters of the Heart
"I'm Going To Be a… What?!"

*Sons of Texas
†Daughters of Texas
††Secret Sisters
◊The Crenshaws of Texas

ANNETTE BROADRICK

believes in romance and the magic of life. Since 1984, Annette has shared her view of life and love with readers. In addition to being nominated by *Romantic Times* magazine as one of the Best New Authors of that year, she has also won the *Romantic Times* Reviewers' Choice Award for Best in its Series, the *Romantic Times* WISH Award, and the *Romantic Times* magazine Lifetime Achievement Awards for Series Romance and Series Romantic Fantasy.

Prologue

It was mid-October. The Crenshaws of Texas were having a party, and everyone for miles around had been invited.

Joe and Gail Crenshaw's oldest son, Jake, and Ashley—the only child of Joe's foreman, Kenneth Sullivan—had been married in a private ceremony earlier in the day and now all their friends and neighbors were celebrating at one of Joe's famous barbecues.

Strings of lights decorated the large live oaks surrounding the hacienda-style homestead, and dozens of tiki torches offered light to the crowd and discouraged any lingering mosquitoes that might have survived the first cold front that had moved through the Hill Country of Texas the week before.

The patio had been cleared for dancing to the music of a local country-western band, and people of all ages were either dancing or watching those who were.

Heather—Jake's four-year-old daughter from his first marriage—raced in and around the visitors with Blackie, her three-month-old Border collie puppy, nipping at her heels. A half-dozen children followed them, sounding like a noisy uprising from the kindergarten set.

Joe and Gail watched the festivities from a picnic table near the patio. Gail chuckled at the children's antics. Life had certainly changed for them during the past few months since Jake discovered he had a daughter. At long last, Gail was a grandmother. She couldn't have been happier.

"I'm so glad to see Heather playing with the other children. It's quite a change from her birthday party three weeks ago. She wouldn't leave Jake's arms all evening."

"I think having the puppy has helped her overcome her shyness." Joe looked at the people milling around. "Looks like everyone's enjoying tonight. I'm glad the weather cooperated."

Gail laughed. "We've never had bad weather on the day of one of our parties. Have you noticed that?"

"I just figured that's what you wanted, so I did what I could to please you."

She snickered. "You are so full of it." She leaned over and gave him a quick kiss. "I sometimes wonder why I've put up with you all these years."

He pulled her close and nuzzled her ear. "You want me to remind you?" he asked silkily, causing her to blush.

She immediately changed the subject before his comments continued.

"I'm glad Jake and Ashley agreed to have a short engagement. Heather wanted Ashley living with them as soon as they told her they were to marry." She searched for the couple until she spotted them dancing. "It's been wonderful to see Jake happy again after all those years alone."

The band was playing a slow tune and they watched as Jake and Ashley swayed together, their arms firmly wrapped around each other.

Joe looked around, wondering where his three younger sons were hiding. "I hope the others decide to follow Jake's lead and settle down one of these days."

He spotted them in the shadows of one of the large trees, watching the festivities from a safe distance.

Joe loved his sons, although they'd been a handful to bring up. What one didn't think of to do, another one would. High-spirited, Gail called them. Joe thought of them as rambunctious and rowdy.

He had to admit that they hadn't turned out half-bad. In fact, he was downright proud of them.

He and Gail had been stunned when Jason, their youngest son, showed up unexpectedly at the ranch yesterday. He'd made the Army his career and now had a highly classified, and dangerous, position in Special Ops.

Jude, their third son, had been part of the National Security Agency for the past three years. At present, he was working out of San Antonio on some kind of classified assignment. Joe had long ago learned not to inquire into his two younger sons' work. He was pleased that Jude had been close enough to come to the wedding.

Jared was the one he tended to worry about. He'd always had a strong independent streak. He had a degree in petroleum engineering and was hired by one of the largest oil companies in the world as soon as he graduated. He seemed to enjoy his job as troubleshooter for the company, traveling from one hot spot to another around the world. He had just returned from Saudi Arabia.

Joe knew that Jared was good at what he did. He should know—Jared had found oil on the ranch the summer before his senior year at the University of Texas. But Joe worried that Jared courted danger wherever he went. Almost a daredevil. Either that or he was convinced he was immortal. He'd always taken too many chances, ever since he was a child.

He couldn't see Jared settling down anytime soon.

Gail smiled as she saw her three younger sons catching up on each other's lives. It had been a long while since all four of the boys had been anywhere at the same time.

The Crenshaw males were tall and blond with a rangy build that made them look good in whatever they chose to wear. They had broad, muscular shoulders and chests, narrow waists, long legs and what Gail thought of as snake hips. Shopping for them when they were kids had been a chore, trying to find pants that would fit their narrow waists and hips and long legs.

All of them had Joe's looks and charisma, the same kind of looks and charisma that had caught her attention so many years ago. She'd fallen hard for the man and had never once regretted jumping into marriage soon after they met.

"It's good to have all four of them home at the same time," Joe said, echoing Gail's thoughts.

"I consider it a miracle," Gail softly replied.

"Great party…as usual," one of their neighbors said, sitting down across from them. "I swear, you two don't look old enough to have four strapping sons. Life certainly agrees with you."

Joe looked at Gail with a lifted brow and a provocative smile, causing her to blush before they both laughed.

"I have to agree with you there, Stu," Joe replied.

* * *

"Hey, Jared," Jason said. With a nod toward two new arrivals, he asked, "Do you know the couple who just arrived? She's quite a looker."

Jared glanced over his shoulder, saw the couple Jason was talking about and did a double take.

"Well, I'll be."

"What?" Jude asked.

"That's Senator Russell."

"Really," Jason replied. "Why would a U.S. senator be coming to one of our parties?"

Jared took a sip of beer from the long-necked bottle in his hand. "Good question. We know that the family's been working on obtaining better water rights. The good senator heads up one of the committees that will decide whether the bill that was recently introduced will get out of committee and onto the floor. Maybe Dad thinks a casual meeting between the interested parties and Russell might help things along."

All three of them watched the couple being greeted by several well-wishers. Senator Russell was an imposing figure, tall and lean with thick silvery hair brushed away from his forehead. The senator's deep voice carried even from this distance. No doubt about it, the man had charisma and a winning smile.

"Is that his wife?" Jason finally asked.

Jared hadn't taken his eyes off the young woman since her arrival. "Not a wife. He's been a widower for years. I wonder if that's his daughter?"

The woman with Senator Russell wore her dark hair pulled away from her face in some kind of fancy twist. He had to admit the hairdo revealed an exquisite profile. She looked expensive, which wasn't surprising given the senator's fortune, and shook hands like royalty graciously greeting her subjects.

He smiled. Miss Royalty. Yeah, that suited her.

Jared glanced at his brothers and grinned. "If you two will excuse me, I believe I'll go introduce myself, maybe help entertain her while she's here."

"And at least get a phone number. If you strike out, maybe Jude or I will have a chance," Jason said.

Jared strode away from his brothers, their knowing chuckles following him.

A Texas barbecue was nothing like the formal parties Lindsey Russell attended with her father in Washington. She smiled at the obvious enjoyment of the guests. The mixture of music, simultaneous conversations and uproarious laughter at the Crenshaw party was a far cry from what she was used to, and she felt a little overwhelmed.

She hadn't been in Texas for several years. She hadn't even accompanied her father when he returned from time to time to meet with constituents. Instead, she'd stayed in Washington, attending a series of private schools and most recently Georgetown University, from which she'd graduated this past June.

Only then did Lindsey understand that her father planned for her to stay in Washington to be available to act as his hostess for various dinners and other occasions.

Her father had been amused that she'd chosen to major in art history, saying it didn't really matter, since she wouldn't ever have to make a living for herself. He intended to support her until she married. He would, of course, make certain any prospective husband had the means to keep her in the style to which she was accustomed.

For the past three years, Lindsey had sincerely hoped

that her father might marry one of the ladies he escorted around town so that he would switch his focus off her. However, there had been no sign that he was anything more than friends with the women, and Lindsey had begun to despair that he would ever step back and allow her to live her own life and to make her own decisions.

He ignored her when she attempted to tell him that she wasn't interested in getting married anytime soon. Her present goal was to get out on her own, get a job, support herself and not have him micromanaging her life.

Her father was like a mother hen with one chick, constantly hovering over her and insisting that he knew what was best for her.

She'd done what she could to keep him happy by working hard at school and making good grades. She'd even acquiesced when her dad had wanted her to live at home and attend Georgetown rather than Vassar, the school of her choice.

Lindsey had now taken a stand and he didn't like it. He didn't like it at all. She'd hoped that by spending these past several months after graduation with him he would be more agreeable to her plans to leave home.

How naive could she possibly have been? In retrospect, she should have known that because she had gone along with his plans for her for all of her life, he wasn't going to let go of any decision-making where she was concerned.

Hence, their rather noisy altercation earlier today.

For the past two weeks she'd been in New York visiting with one of her college friends, Janeen White. She and Janeen had met in the Art History department and had immediately bonded when Janeen explained that she had chosen to attend Georgetown U to get away from her well-meaning—but meddling—family in New York.

Janeen's family was comfortably wealthy and moved in the best circles. Her parents, like the senator, felt that they knew what was best for Janeen. Unlike Lindsey, Janeen had stood up to them and had moved to Washington despite their protests.

During her four years away from home Janeen set necessary boundaries where her family was concerned. Now that she had her degree, she had gotten her own apartment in Manhattan and worked full-time at the Metropolitan Museum of Art, where she'd interned during the past three summers.

Because of Janeen, Lindsey had gotten an interview with the curator of the museum while she was visiting Janeen in New York. Lindsey had been ecstatic when the curator offered to hire her as an assistant to one of the assistants at the museum starting in January.

Lindsey couldn't contain her excitement. She'd arrived at her father's ranch late last night and announced over breakfast that she would be moving to New York the first of the year.

Her father's reaction could have been heard in the three surrounding states and Mexico. Lindsey had never seen him so upset. Then again, she'd never defied him before.

She'd stood up to him, but staying calm and not giving in to angry tears had been the toughest things she'd ever faced. She still trembled when she recalled the scene.

"What do you mean, you've accepted a job in New York? Are you out of your mind?" he'd said, slapping the table with his open hand. Thank goodness they'd finished eating and there was little remaining liquid in their water and orange juice glasses, although one of their cups of coffee had overturned.

He ignored the mess and glared at her.

"You know, Dad," she replied in a calm voice, "I could better understand your reaction if I were sixteen years old and had just announced that I was running off with the elephant trainer in a circus, but the fact is that I'm twenty-five years old. Most people my age have been working for years."

"You're not most people, Lindsey. You are my daughter and there is absolutely no reason for you to take a job, especially as a lowly assistant to another lowly assistant. It's demeaning, is what it is."

In a patient voice, she said, "I would willingly pay them for the opportunity to work at the museum, Dad. I'll be learning from experts and will get the best training possible in my field."

"Your field," he said with a sneer. "Dabbling in art history certainly doesn't count as a professional field!"

"Further," she continued, without losing eye contact, "if and when I marry, I will be the one to decide who will be the groom—not you, not your friends with eligible sons, not the winning ticket holder of some bizarre society raffle."

He stood and glared at her. "You are being insubordinate and I will not tolerate it. Do you understand me?"

She stood, as well, unobtrusively leaning against the table to steady her shaking knees.

"Did you hear what you just said? You've just proved my point. Only a subordinate can be insubordinate and I am not one of your underlings."

"You owe me respect, young lady, and I'm not seeing any respect in your attitude this morning."

"Of course I respect you. I always have. The problem has been that this is the first time I haven't backed down when you've decided my next course of action."

"Damn it, child! I didn't put you in all those fancy boarding and finishing schools for you to defy me now! What happened to the sweet, biddable young woman I love?"

Lindsey sighed. "She grew up, Dad." She'd turned away and started toward her room when he said, "Your mother would be horrified that you'd want to live alone in New York City, absolutely horrified."

She'd been waiting for that one, one of many guilt trips he used on her to get her to do what he wanted.

Lindsey turned in the doorway and faced him. "You know, Dad, I've heard variations on that remark most of my life and it's been used to death. I have no idea what my mother would have wanted for me at this stage in my life. But neither do you.

"Mother has been gone for seventeen years and I'm no longer that eight-year-old child you were left to rear. The world has changed considerably during those years. And so have I. I love you, never forget that, but I'm an adult now. I'm perfectly capable of looking after myself without your help. Regardless of what you say, I am moving to New York in January."

His face flushed an unhealthy red as he said, "This discussion in not over, whether you walk out of this room or not."

At least he'd put her on notice that their home would be a battleground for the rest of the year.

It was true she didn't have to work. She'd received the trust account from her mother's estate last spring, much to her father's irritation, which made moot his threat of cutting off her funds when she didn't do as he wanted.

There was nothing more he could threaten her with and her newfound sense of freedom was an overwhelming relief.

He could throw all kinds of fits from now on and she wouldn't change her plans. So, okay, maybe she'd come tonight to help ease the tension between them. Attending the party of a family whose financial support had helped to put her father into the U.S. Senate was easy enough for her to do, even when she didn't know anyone there.

Children darted in and out of the crowd and she noted that most of the older men were congregated near the barbecue pit, laughing and talking, while the older women visited among themselves.

The women her age all had dates.

She felt a little out of place, being there with her father. Lindsey knew how to mingle with statesmen and royalty with aplomb, but she'd never learned to mingle with Texas cowboys and ranchers, and their wives and girlfriends.

The Crenshaw home surprised her. Built on the lines of the haciendas constructed in the previous century, the adobe walls and red-tiled roof looked like something out of a movie. The large patio was surrounded by native shrubbery and the wide lawn appeared to be the perfect place to have a party.

Everyone in Texas had heard of the Crenshaw family, whose holdings in the Hill Country were probably the size of Rhode Island. Or larger. Her father told her that the land had been in the Crenshaw family for several generations.

Lindsey's thoughts were interrupted when her dad spoke. "There's some people here I need to speak to," he said, smiling at her as though they hadn't been arguing off and on all day. "You'd be bored tagging along with me. Why don't you join that group of ladies over there and get to know some of these people."

He didn't wait for her response. She watched him make his way through the crowd, smiling, shaking hands, being slapped on the back. He was in his element while she was definitely the outsider. She glanced at the ladies to whom he'd referred. The youngest one appeared to be in her mid-fifties.

"Good evening, ma'am," a deep voice drawled from somewhere nearby. "I don't believe we've met."

Lindsey turned to see who had spoken to her. Oh, my. Here was a man who radiated self-confidence...and for good reason. Tall, blond, broad-shouldered and lean-hipped, the man personified all the mystique and wonder of Texas, with a flashing smile in a bronze-colored face and eyes so blue she could swim in them.

He probably knew his impact on women, but the knowledge in no way detracted from his charm.

Her heart picked up its rhythm and she smiled, more at her reaction than at the man. There was something about a good-looking man in tight jeans that attracted her more than all the men in suits and ties she'd been around most of her life.

He held out his hand and she placed hers in his much larger one.

"I'm Jared Crenshaw," he said, placing his other hand over hers in a proprietary way. "And you must be—" He paused, his smile broadening into a grin.

Hmm. Jared Crenshaw could definitely be a hazard to her peace of mind.

"Lindsey Russell," she said, matching his grin. So he was a Crenshaw, was he? No wonder he appeared self-confident. Not only did he have money and prestige behind him, his blond good looks would have been enough to attract any woman he wanted.

"I'm pleased to meet you, Mr. Crenshaw. You're the first member of your family I've met."

He stared deeply into her eyes. "Mr. Crenshaw happens to be my dad. Please call me Jared."

She gently tugged her hand from his clasp. "I don't know you well enough to be quite so familiar."

He grinned wickedly at her and she knew his thoughts as though he'd spoken them aloud. Lindsey blushed, hoping he hadn't noticed. She'd never before been so aware of a man.

What a darling. Jared hadn't seen a grown woman blush before.

He liked the look of her—her expressive eyes surrounded by thick lashes, her slow smile, as though she hadn't had much to smile about lately, her trim body and the fact that her head barely reached his shoulders.

Jared didn't usually go for the type. As a rule, he preferred tall, buxom blondes who were eager to spend time with him with absolutely no strings attached. The fact was, Jared enjoyed women…women of all kinds. He just wasn't interested in marrying one of them anytime soon.

The senator's daughter was different from the others he knew and he sort of liked the difference. Her beauty was more subtle, maybe, but every bit as impressive.

"Then we need to do something to make you feel more familiar with me," he said, and was rewarded by another blush. He offered his hand to her, palm up, and said, "Let me introduce you around."

He waited to see what she would do. He was teasing her, hoping to break down some of that reserve that seemed to surround her, and he wondered if she would get it.

He could see the debate running through her mind—uncertain how to handle him but not wanting to appear rude.

Her upbringing won out and she placed her hand in his. He almost hugged her. What a darling.

"Probably half the people here are kinfolk of mine." Jared winked. "Of course, none of them are as good-looking." She looked at him in astonishment and he burst out laughing. "I'm teasing, honestly. Guess you'll have to get used to my sense of humor." If he had anything to do with it, she'd have plenty of chances to be around him. He didn't care if she was a senator's daughter, he just wanted to spend some time with her.

Lindsey didn't know how to take Jared's remarks. He could have been teasing, or he could be insufferably smug.

The jury was still out on that one.

"Hope you haven't eaten lately," he said, as they walked across the lawn toward the crowd. "Dad makes the best barbecue you've ever tasted."

Lindsey didn't particularly like barbecue, but she saw no reason to mention it. "I'm not very hungry," she said, trying to walk a thin line between being polite and being honest, "but of course I'll try some."

He kept staring at her, his gaze wandering across her face, and she wondered if there was a smudge on her nose or something. "Is something wrong?" she finally asked.

He grinned. "No, ma'am, there's not a thing wrong with you. In fact, you are one fine-looking lady. You know, I'm surprised I've never seen you before," he continued. "Doesn't your dad own a ranch the other side of New Eden?"

"Yes, but I've spent very little time there. I went to school back East and most of my friends live there."

"It's our loss, I guess." His eyes danced and she knew he was teasing her again.

"What do you mean?"

"All the guys who live around here. Just remember, though. I saw you first!"

She stopped in her tracks. "That sounds like you intend to brand me with your initials or something."

He burst into laughter. "Wouldn't have thought of that, but it sounds like a fine idea to me."

She gave him a withering look—which, she noted, didn't faze him—and said, "In your dreams, cowboy."

He was still laughing when they arrived at a long table weighed down by enough food to feed an army—a very large army, at that. There was a short line of people helping themselves to various items, such as beans and potato salad, coleslaw and all kinds of desserts. At the end of the table a couple of men placed barbecue on the guests' plates.

Although she took small portions of each item, by the time Lindsey received a large slice of beef and several pork ribs, her plate was piled high with food. She would never be able to eat even half of it.

Jared was right behind her and his plate was equally laden. He nodded to one of the tables. "That's my folks over there. C'mon. We can sit at their table and I'll introduce them to you."

What an impression she was going to make. Her plate looked as though she was starving. Lindsey couldn't remember a time when she'd been so uncomfortable. All the rules of etiquette that had been drilled into her didn't seem to cover this situation.

Once they were seated, Jared said, "Mom, Dad, I want you to meet Lindsey Russell, the senator's daughter." He smiled at Lindsey. "Joe and Gail Crenshaw."

"How do you do?" she said with a nod and a smile.

"This woman has been seriously deprived," Jared said seriously. "She hasn't seen much of Texas and she's never been to one of our barbecues. I'm going to do my best to make up for that."

Lindsey looked at him in astonishment.

"Don't pay any attention to him," Gail Crenshaw said. "He'd rather tease than eat." She paused and looked at him attack his plate. "Well, maybe it's more of a tie, actually. I'm so pleased to meet you, Lindsey. Your mother and I were classmates and friends. I know she'd be delighted to see how well you turned out."

Lindsey placed her fork on her plate. "You knew her?" she asked wonderingly.

"Yes, our fathers were good friends and she and I spent a lot of our growing-up years together, then she went to a private high school back East and we got out of touch for a while. After she married and moved back here with your father, we got together once in a while for a visit."

"I don't remember any of that."

"Probably not. Your roots grow deep here in the Hill Country, you know."

"I'd like to talk to you sometime about her. There's so much I want to know about her but it makes my dad depressed whenever I bring her up in conversation, so I stopped asking about her."

"I'd like that, Lindsey. Call whenever your schedule's free and we'll get together."

"Speaking of calling," Jared said, "could I have your phone number? Only the senator's Texas office is listed in the phone book. Guess he doesn't want to be bothered at home."

She looked at him, sitting there beside her. "My phone number?"

"Don't act so surprised," he said. "If I'm going to teach you about all things Texan, I'm going to have to spend some time with you, right? I know it will be a hardship on me, having to see you so much, but hey, I'm man enough to handle it."

When both of his parents erupted into laughter, Lindsey realized that once again he'd been teasing her. He was so different from the young men she'd known, and she had trouble knowing how to deal with him.

"Well," she finally said, "I suppose I can give you my phone number, all in the interest of Texas patriotism, of course."

Joe looked at Jared and said, "I think she's already got your number, son. She can obviously handle anything you dish out."

By the time she'd finished her meal, Lindsey had grown comfortable with the three Crenshaws. She was amused at how his parents sided with her when Jared attempted to give her a hard time. She couldn't remember when she'd laughed so much. They were friendly and down-to-earth. Plus, Jared's mom had known her mom, which automatically made Lindsey feel closer to the older woman.

Jared leaned toward her, close enough for her to smell his aftershave lotion, and asked, "Care to dance?"

Lindsey looked over her shoulder at the dancers crowding the patio.

"I don't think so, but thank you. I don't know any of those dances."

"Then this is as good a time as any to begin your education regarding the culture of Texas." He held out his hand with a slight bow. "May I have the honor of this dance, Your Highness?"

"What did you call me?"

He grinned. "Your well-bred manners remind me of royalty."

"I'm stuffy?"

Gail and Joe laughed.

"Nope. You are regal. I like that in a woman."

She took his hand. "How can a woman possibly turn down such a flattering request," she replied, mimicking the reserved, haughty speaking style of the headmistress at her academy. She turned to Joe and Gail, "I've enjoyed visiting with you. I'll give you a call soon so we can talk," she added to Gail.

Lindsey caught on quickly to the two-step, the cotton-eyed joe and the moves in line dancing. She couldn't remember when she'd had so much fun. Many of her inhibitions slipped away during the rest of the evening, as she danced with first one and then another male despite Jared's mocking growl.

He was funny. His "just a country boy" demeanor couldn't hide his intelligence and his enthusiasm for his chosen profession, which impressed her. He probably didn't need to work for the rest of his life and yet he'd found a field he enjoyed.

Just as she had. How could she not admire his ambition?

She caught a glimpse of her father from time to time, obviously delighted to see her dancing and having fun. She felt mellower about his bullheadedness. He loved her. She knew that without a doubt. Sooner or later he would accept her decision to live her own life. She would learn to be more patient with him. After all, she was the only family he had. He probably needed her more than she needed him at this stage in their lives.

Eventually, the hour grew late and the number of dancers on the floor dwindled. The band played ballads and Jared held her close, both arms around her waist. Lindsey wasn't used to being held quite so closely, but when she glanced around at the other dancers, she saw that the men held their partners as Jared was holding her and the women danced with their arms around the men's neck.

Because Jared was so much taller than her, Lindsey's hands rested on his chest.

"I'm really glad you came to our party," Jared said. "I

wish I'd met you years ago. Of course you'd have been much too young to date me back then."

She leaned back a little. "How old do you think I am?"

He stared intently at her and said, "Twenty-one. Maybe."

"Twenty-five."

"No kidding. Well, I've still got six years on you. If you'd gone to school here, you would have been in the sixth grade when I graduated from high school. So maybe this is the perfect time for us to meet."

She could practically feel his shirt buttons pressing against her. During one of their turns, his leg somehow moved between hers. The gentle friction not only aroused her but him, as well, his jeans unable to camouflage his reaction to her.

So why wasn't she pushing herself away from him? She'd never allowed anyone to hold her in such a way. For the very first time in her life, Lindsey was discovering a sensuous side to her nature, one she'd had no idea existed.

Jared Crenshaw was teaching her much more than he suspected, and she felt vulnerable. She'd always considered herself to be a rational and logical person. Now the feelings he stirred in her confused her. Not that she thought he had any long-term plans where she was concerned. A couple of the men who'd danced with her had quickly informed her that Jared Crenshaw definitely played the field.

Actually, she found their comments reassuring. The last thing she needed was to begin a serious relationship with someone in Texas when she planned to move to New York. She certainly might consider seeing him while she was in Texas, knowing that he wasn't looking for a committed relationship.

Let's face it—she enjoyed his company, and he appeared to enjoy hers. They were adults. Why shouldn't they spend some time together?

The song stopped and the band took a break.

"You've been awfully quiet, you know," Jared said as he stepped away from her. "Bored, already?"

She smiled and shook her head. "On the contrary, Mr. Crenshaw," she said mockingly, "I can't remember when I've had quite so much fun."

"Mr. Crenshaw, huh," he growled in fake menace. He took her hand and pulled her around the corner from the patio and into the shadows of a large bush. Before she knew what he was up to, he cupped her face in his hands and said, "Guess I'm going to have to do something about your calling me mister." He lowered his lips to hers and pressed gently against them.

Lindsey could have easily stepped away from him, but she discovered that she didn't want to. In fact, she went up on her toes and kissed him back. He made a slight sound and deepened the kiss.

Dazed by the immediate assault on her emotions, Lindsey could only sigh with pleasure. She was no connoisseur of kissing, but in her opinion, Jared had mastered it. By the time he reluctantly lifted his head, her head was spinning.

"What is my name?" he whispered.

She smiled. "Jared."

"That's right. Although I was hoping you might need more convincing."

"Oh, I'm definitely convinced. I'll never think of you as Mr. Crenshaw again."

He grinned. "Good. One of my goals accomplished."

"One of them?"

"You don't think I'm going to give away all my secrets, do you?"

"Is this part of my learning the culture of Texas?"

He burst into laughter. "You're too much, Lindsey Russell. I can't tell you how delighted I am you came to the party tonight."

"I've enjoyed it." She looked around. "But don't you think we should stop hiding in the bushes?"

"I suppose. If you insist."

"I insist."

He took her hand and pulled her close to him. "Let's get something to drink. I need to cool off a little." He glanced at her out of the corner of his eye. "From the dancing, you know."

"Of course," she said, hoping to sound innocent of his real meaning.

They found a couple of lawn chairs after they got their drinks and sat facing the dancers. Lindsey glanced at the hacienda, amazed at its size.

"Do you live here?" she asked.

He looked at the house. "Probably the whole family could live here and seldom run into each other, but no, only my brother Jake and his wife live here now. Various Crenshaws have homes scattered all across our land, whether they work it or just live on it. Mom and Dad built a smaller place about five miles away several years ago. And if you follow the ranch road over there, there's a settlement of homes for all the workers. Some of them are descendants from the original families that worked for Jeremiah Calhoun, the founder of the clan.

"I've been staying in one of the houses built for our married workers because it happened to be empty. It's plenty big for me, and furnished, which helps."

"And I suppose you do your own cooking?" she asked, teasing him.

"Not so you'd notice," he replied with a slow drawl.

"You mentioned earlier that you've been working in Saudi Arabia. What will you do now?"

"Rest. I help Jake around the ranch, just to keep my hand in. I love the place, I guess we all do, but I get too restless when I stay in one place too long." He shifted so that he could face her. "How about you? You said you'd gotten your degree. What do you intend to do with it?"

With renewed excitement, she said, "Starting in January I'll be working at the Metropolitan Museum of Art in New York City."

"No kidding! How did you manage that right out of college?"

"It's who you know, of course."

"Your dad?"

"Heavens, no. If he had his way I'd never leave home."

"A little possessive, is he?"

Lindsey was having trouble keeping her mind on their discussion. The look in his blue eyes suggested that he, too, was not paying much attention to their verbal communication. The expression of his heated gaze made it clear what he would prefer to be doing at the moment, which was why they were sitting in plain view of everyone, she was sure.

If she felt a certain disappointment that he wouldn't be kissing her again, she had to agree that he'd made the right choice.

"Dad's okay, but I don't particularly want to talk about him."

He sipped his drink. "Me, either. I'd much rather talk about you."

"Then you're going to be quickly bored because I've given you my entire life history in one evening."

"Oh, I imagine there's a few things you've neglected to mention."

"Such as?"

"A fiancé, a boyfriend, maybe several?" He lifted his brows inquiringly.

"Oh, is this where we swap stories about our love life?"

"Not on your life. I just want to know if I'm poaching, that's all."

"Poaching?" She shook her head. "Your Texas idioms sometimes catch me off guard."

"And you're avoiding the question."

She folded her hands and primly replied, "I am not dating anyone at the moment."

"Good."

"However, I don't intend to get serious about anyone for a long, long time."

"Good," he repeated, and she burst into laughter. "So let me have your phone number and I'll be in touch. You need to learn something about your history here in the Lone Star State and I'm just the fella to teach you."

She reached into her purse and found a piece of paper. After printing the numbers for her home phone and her cell phone, she handed it to him.

He nodded, carefully folded it and put it in his wallet.

Later, when Lindsey and her father were on their way home, her dad said, "I was pleased to see you enjoying yourself tonight, sweetheart. I noticed one of the Crenshaw boys fairly monopolized you all evening. Which one was he? I get them confused."

"Jared." She didn't want to talk. She wanted to close her eyes and relive the evening from the time Jared had first introduced himself.

"Ah. He's the petroleum engineer, I believe."

"Uh-huh."

"Someone mentioned that Jared recently returned from the Middle East."

"That's right."

They drove for several miles in silence, each lost in thought, until her father broke the silence by saying, "You know, Lindsey, you could do a lot worse than to snag a Crenshaw. They have a great deal of influence in this state."

She turned and looked at her father. The soft glow from the dashboard of the luxury car revealed his face enough for her to tell that he wasn't joking.

Regardless, Lindsey tried to make light of his remark. "I only danced with Jared tonight, Dad. I didn't offer to have his baby." She blushed, though, at the thought.

"Do you intend to see him again?"

"Maybe. He said he'd call."

"Good." Her father looked quite satisfied with her answer. Then she understood his pleased expression.

"Whether or not I go out with Jared, I'm moving to Manhattan in January."

He didn't say anything right away. When he did, he sounded casual. "Well, January's still a couple of months away. Lots can happen between now and then."

She closed her eyes. She would be hearing variations on that theme until the day she moved to New York, so she might as well learn not to rise to the bait.

One

Three weeks later…

Jared abruptly came awake at the sound of a crashing door.

At that moment, he was aware of only two things—he had the mother of all hangovers, and the door to his bedroom had flown open hard enough to bounce off the wall.

Since he lived alone, there was no reason for anyone to come charging into the room.

He painfully squinted his eyes open and discovered that the pounding in his head was the least of his problems.

This wasn't his bedroom.

Where the hell was he? He stared at the lace-edged canopy above him before slowly moving his gaze around the rest of the room. *His* bedroom sure as hell didn't smell like flowers or contain this delicate furniture.

He stared at a wall of shelves filled with fancy-dressed dolls before he closed his eyes again.

Maybe the hangover was affecting his vision. He softly massaged his eyes, hoping to improve his sight. When he opened them again, he flinched.

Two men stood just inside the doorway.

Two very angry-looking men.

That explained a lot. He was having a nightmare, that's what it was. He was in the midst of a dream where he went to bed in his own room and woke up in what looked to be a female's bedroom.

If he wasn't dreaming, then he must have died and gone straight to hell. He could think of no other reason why his father would be standing by the doorway next to Senator Russell.

Lindsey Russell's father.

Lindsey Russell's father!

What the—?

Jared turned his head and then grabbed it before it tumbled off his shoulders. Somehow he should have known whom he would find, even though he was having great difficulty comprehending any of this.

Lindsey Russell lay next to him, facing him, with one hand tucked beneath her cheek. How could she possibly be asleep after the racket their fathers had just made?

There was no denying that he was in a heap of trouble. Big-time trouble. Whatever was going on—and he didn't have a clue what he was doing in Lindsey's bed—was going to be damn hard to explain.

He knew what their visitors thought, of course—the same thing he would have thought in their place.

At the moment, he could barely wrap his mind around the fact that at some point last night he must have gone to bed with Lindsey. How could that be? They'd been seeing each other, sure, but he'd known from the very beginning of their relationship that she wouldn't sleep with him. He'd continued to see her, anyway, willing to spend as much time with her as she would allow.

He liked her. He liked her a lot. Hell, if she'd given him any sign that she would take the next step, he would have been all for it.

Is that what happened last night?

If so, why couldn't he remember any of it?

He tried to recall the night before. He was fairly certain they hadn't planned to see each other. He'd worked with Jake all day doing hard, physical labor. As a matter of fact, his aching muscles this morning were already protesting against being used so strenuously.

He recalled getting cleaned up at his place and going into town for something to eat.

Jared scrubbed his hand roughly through his hair in an effort to make his brain wake up.

While at the Mustang Bar & Grill in New Eden—the closest town to the ranch—he'd run into Matt and Denny, a couple of guys he'd grown up with. Once he was through with dinner, he'd decided to stay a while and shoot some pool with them.

When did he start drinking heavily enough to cause such a painful morning after? Enough so that he couldn't remember the rest of the evening? Because he couldn't remember a single, solitary thing after that.

All of this flashed through his mind in the time it took him to register where he was. He stared at the men, who stared back, looking at him as though he were pond scum.

And why not? The situation couldn't have put him in a worse light.

Jared pushed himself up, rested his elbows on his bent knees and held his head. "I can explain—" he said slowly, his voice the sound of a croaking bullfrog. He cleared his throat. "You see," he said, and then paused. He looked at his dad, who now leaned against the door jamb with his arms crossed and one booted foot across the other. Next, he glanced at Lindsey who had stirred at the sound of his voice. "Actually," he continued, "I have no idea how I got here or why I'm here."

His gaze kept going back to Lindsey, who looked amazingly pretty first thing in the morning, her face slightly flushed with sleep, her dark hair tumbled around her shoulders and draped across her pillow.

He forced his gaze back to the men.

Joe lifted an eyebrow. "Oh, I think R.W. and I can figure out that last one without any explanation on your part," Joe drawled softly.

Jared winced. He respected his father more than any man he knew, but the thing about his father was, the lower and softer his dad spoke, the angrier he was. And, oh boy, was Joe Crenshaw ever angry at this particular moment!

Lindsey shifted and his gaze immediately sought her out. She sat up and held the covers to her shoulders, looking at him in sleepy astonishment, her eyes wide.

"Jared?" she said, sounding incredulous. "What in the world are you doing here?"

He cleared his throat again. "I—uh—was kind of hoping you could tell me."

Only then did Lindsey become aware of the men at her door. "Oh, my gosh!" she said faintly, turning fiery red. "What's going on here?"

He understood her stunned reaction perfectly since it mirrored his own. However, he was more bewildered than ever. Her shock was genuine. She was as surprised as he was to find them in bed together.

And their situation certainly wasn't being helped by their fathers' presence.

He reached toward her, trying to think of something to say, but his dad spoke first.

"I suggest that you get dressed, Jared, and we'll deal with this later."

Senator Russell spoke for the first time since they'd entered the room, his voice shaking with rage. "We'll deal with it now, Joe. The only thing that needs to be decided at the moment is a date for the wedding. And from the looks of things, it had better be soon!"

"Marriage!" Jared yelped, then groaned and held his aching head.

Lindsey stiffened and glared at the three men.

"Absolutely not! I will not take part in any marriage, so don't even think about it." With regal dignity, Lindsey picked up her robe and pulled it on over her nightgown, tying it at her waist. Then she stood and walked across the room to her bathroom as though the men no longer existed.

She closed the door quietly behind her.

Jared had had enough of this farce. He swung his feet to the floor, causing his stomach to roil. Oh, just what he needed—to hurl, in addition to everything else that had happened.

He dropped his head into his hands and groaned.

Finally, he said, "I don't know what's going on here, or how I got here, but I swear to you both that I never touched her."

"How do you know what you did if you don't remember how you got here?" Lindsey's father said with a sneer.

Jared straightened and met the man's gaze. "Because I

wouldn't take advantage of Lindsey in that way. I know that. She knows that. Besides, you heard her. She was just as surprised as I am to find me here." He paused for a moment, studying the men. "As far as that goes, I don't understand what the two of you are doing here. Lindsey and I are both adults and it's nobody's business whether we slept together or not."

Joe shook his head and turned away. "Get some clothes on," he said over his shoulder, "and then we'll talk."

He left the room.

Jared looked around for his clothes. They were scattered on the floor as if he'd been in a hurry to get undressed. He'd taken off everything but his boxer shorts. That was small consolation, but at the moment, he'd accept anything.

Had he made love to her, neither one of them would have had clothes on. He knew that for sure. Before she'd pulled her robe on, he'd gotten a glimpse of Lindsey's cotton nightgown and felt a real sense of relief. Regardless of how he'd managed to turn up in Lindsey's bed, he hadn't taken advantage of her.

With a stirring of determination, Jared shoved his feet into his jeans and pulled them up as he stood, his head still spinning and pounding so hard he felt like he was going to pass out. Ignoring Senator Russell, Jared pulled on his socks, boots and shirt, picked up his hat and stalked out of the bedroom.

Joe was waiting for him in the living room. Jared hoped never again to see such a look of contempt aimed at him from his dad.

"I'm really disappointed in you, Jared," Joe said softly. "I have never said a word to you about your social life because you're right, it's none of my business. At the same time, I never would have thought a son of mine would seduce an innocent girl and then pretend he can't remember anything about it. You've disgraced the family name, Jared—there's no two ways about it. In case you want to know my feelings on the matter, I'll tell you this—if R.W. thinks there should be a wedding, then it would behoove you to polish up your dress boots and make certain you have a suit cleaned, because there *will* be a wedding if I have anything to say about it."

"That sounds like a threat," Jared replied slowly, holding his gaze steady. "And whatever you think about me or my behavior, I know without a doubt that I did nothing to harm Lindsey last night. Not one thing. There was no seduction, no betrayal of her. And I'll be damned if I'm going to let you or anyone else railroad me into a marriage that neither Lindsey nor I want."

Neither gaze wavered as they continued to stare each other down.

Joe finally looked away and said, "Damn it, Jared! The last thing the Crenshaws need right now is to get sideways with Senator Russell. You know exactly why we need his support on this water rights deal. The last thing we need at this particular time is to make an enemy of him." Joe shook his head wearily. "I wish to hell you'd never seen the senator's daughter!"

"At the moment, I share your sentiment. However, I know that once Lindsey and I have a chance to talk, we'll be able to handle the situation without outside interference. I know her well enough by now to know that she isn't interested in getting married. She's got a job lined up in New York and can hardly wait to move up there.

"She's told me how overprotective her father has always been. If he had his way, he would probably keep her in a convent until he found a husband for her." He glanced down at his feet and the pain in his head intensified drastically. He groaned. "I'd appreciate having this discussion after I've had some coffee and a handful of aspirin. I have a hunch this situation isn't going to be resolved in the next few hours."

"Coffee's in the kitchen," Senator Russell said from somewhere behind him. "I don't know what kind of story you intend to feed us, but the facts speak for themselves, Jared. I woke up this morning and discovered your truck parked outside. When I went looking for you, I'll admit the very last place I expected to find you was in my daughter's bed." He glanced at Joe, then away. "I could kill you for this, just so there's no misunderstanding about how I feel at the moment. In fact, I decided to call Joe before I did bodily harm to you. I wanted him to witness what I had, and I intend to do whatever damage control is necessary, do you understand me?"

Jared took a couple of deep breaths in an attempt to look at all of this from a father's perspective. Especially Lindsey's father's perspective. Finding a man in your single daughter's bed probably wouldn't sit well with any father, but Lindsey's father? Jared was lucky he hadn't been shot while he slept.

In a calm voice, Jared said, "I understand perfectly, sir. If she was my daughter, I'd be feeling the same way."

The senator seemed to relax slightly.

"The problem here is that I consider Lindsey to be a friend. A good friend. She's one of the nicest women I know. There's no way in hell I would have cold-bloodedly seduced her."

Joe narrowed his eyes. "Meaning?"

"I think somebody set me up. For the life of me I can't figure out who would do such a thing, or why. I mean, most everyone in the county knows that I've been seeing her these past few weeks. I certainly haven't kept it a secret. But this is more than a prank. This was malicious and I'm going to find out who did it and what was behind it." He looked at both men. "You can count on that," he said and headed to the kitchen.

Lindsey leaned against the bathroom door, shaking so hard she could scarcely stand. She managed to reach her vanity chair and sank down in front of the mirror. Only then did she realize that tears silently slid down her face.

She had never been so humiliated in her life—first, to wake up to discover Jared Crenshaw in bed with her and second, to have her father bring up the subject of marriage.

She didn't know what to think. She thought she'd gotten to know Jared fairly well. She'd known since the night she'd met him that he found her physically attractive. He'd made no effort to hide his reaction to her whenever they kissed, which was often, but he'd been a perfect gentleman.

Until he'd climbed into her bed!

She shook her head wearily. Who would have dreamed that she would ever be in a position to say, "Guess who's been sleeping in my bed?" but she was neither Goldilocks nor one of the three bears, and this morning was certainly not part of some fairy tale.

The only thing she knew for certain was that Jared had not made love to her. If he had, she would certainly remember it. In fact, she had trouble believing that he could have crawled into bed without waking her.

She wasn't *that* sound a sleeper.

Lindsey absently wrapped her hair into a knot on top of her head and then stepped into the shower.

While she stood under the fine spray she thought about

yesterday. About last night. She'd had a headache that bordered on being a migraine, in no small part due to the fact that she'd again quarreled with her father, threatening to move out this weekend if he said one more word about her moving to New York.

She'd been so angry and frustrated with him that her blood pressure had probably gone off the scales. In her senior year she had seen a doctor about her recurring headaches. He'd given her a prescription for pain medication and suggested that her problem stemmed from stress. No argument there.

Lindsey seldom took the pain pills because they practically knocked her out, but last night she hadn't cared so long as she could get some relief.

Wasn't it a little strange that she should be drugged the night he chose to come to her bed?

Worse than strange.

Unfortunately, she didn't have any answers. What mattered to her at the moment was that her father was carrying on about marriage like some patriarch from a couple of hundred years ago.

Somehow, she'd get through this embarrassing situation. She would attempt to speak with Jared and see what answers he could give her.

Her father would quickly discover that he could not force her into marriage. Unmarried people slept together all the time. It was no big deal. They even had children together without feeling the need to marry. The fact that she'd never had an intimate relationship had nothing to do with him. The choice had been hers to make.

Lindsey dried herself off, dressed and applied some makeup to hide the dark shadows beneath her eyes, part of the remnants of the headache. She left her hair down because a tender scalp was another part of the aftermath of a migraine.

After one last look in the mirror, Lindsey walked out of the bathroom. What she needed now was some coffee.

Jared spotted a small bathroom off the hallway that led to the kitchen. He went inside and splashed water on his face, swearing under his breath when the pain in his head intensified every time he lowered it.

He looked into the mirror and frowned. He looked like he'd been ridden hard and put away wet. He was gray beneath his tan and his blond hair stood out from his scalp in all directions. He rubbed his raspy jaw. It didn't help his appearance any that he definitely needed to shave.

Jared reached into his back pocket and pulled out his comb, wet it and did his best to tame his hair. He could see little improvement in his overall appearance but at least he could now hold his eyes open without wincing from the light.

The kitchen was empty when he walked in. He headed straight to the coffeepot and filled a large mug with the steaming liquid. While he waited for it to cool, Jared opened cabinet doors and drawers in hopes of finding a pain reliever.

"May I help you find something?"

He glanced around and saw Lindsey. Talk about an awkward moment. "I, uh, I was looking for some aspirin tablets." He watched her walk to one of the cabinets he hadn't opened, amazed that she seemed so untouched by the earlier furor.

She reached inside the cabinet and handed him a bottle.

"Thanks."

Next she filled a glass with water and offered it to him, then poured herself a cup of coffee. He downed the pills and watched Lindsey. When she turned, she caught him staring at her.

"Lindsey, I don't know what the hell is going on here, but I would never, not ever, do anything to harm you."

"I guess I'd find that easier to believe if I hadn't found you in bed with me this morning," she replied conversationally. She sipped her coffee.

He winced. "I know it looks bad, but I think too much of you to place you in such an embarrassing situation."

"That's good to know. However, the fact remains that you were in my bed."

"You keep saying that!"

"Only because it's true. I don't know when you arrived. Even though I'd taken pain medicine for my migraine, I can't believe I didn't hear you."

"Look," he said, feeling more than a little testy at the way this conversation was going, "I don't care what you or your dad think, I didn't come over here last night to seduce you."

She looked at him skeptically. "Then what exactly are you doing here?"

He clenched his teeth. "If I knew, I'd tell you, believe me."

After a lengthy pause, she finally asked, "You really don't remember?"

"No." After another long pause, he added, "I was hoping you could tell me what had happened. Guess it was convenient that you were taking stuff for pain."

She looked at him sharply. "What, exactly, is that supposed to mean? Do you think I'd make something like that up?"

"Well, it certainly gives you an out, doesn't it? You slept through the whole thing. You can't be expected to explain my presence, now can you?"

She stared at him for the longest time as though he'd

suddenly grown another head, maybe two. "I don't need to explain anything, Jared. After all, I didn't wake up in *your* bed."

He looked at his watch. "Look, this is going nowhere. I apologize all over the place for ending up here last night. You're no more eager than I am to get married. I've enjoyed your company. Maybe after this blows over, we can continue to see each other until you move."

"You really think this will be forgotten so easily?"

"No. But when they see we have no intention of being pushed into anything, they'll back off."

"Your father may," she said quietly. "Mine won't."

Jared set his cup on the counter and walked over to her.

"You know, Lindsey, if I had planned to make love to you, I would have found a more private place than your bedroom."

She shrugged. "Unless this was some kind of prank you decided to pull. At this point, why you came over makes no difference. Now I have to spend the rest of the day convincing my father not to go after you with a shotgun."

Jared realized that he was wasting his time attempting to explain the inexplicable. He glanced at his watch. "I need to get home and, hopefully, get some sleep. I may need to borrow some of that pain medication you took last night, the way my head feels. I'll check in with you this evening, tomorrow at the latest, to see how you're doing."

She began to shake her head before he finished speaking. "It would be better if you didn't call anymore, Jared. Once it's clear that we're no longer seeing each other, our fathers will be forced to accept that there's nothing serious going on between us."

Jared was surprised to discover that her words bothered him. What was wrong with him, anyway? He'd always known there was nothing going on between them. Maybe he didn't like being dismissed so casually. Maybe his ego was bruised a little.

"Whatever you want to do is okay with me," he finally said. "I just want to say that I've enjoyed getting to know you. We've had some fun times together."

She nodded. "I know."

"If I'm ever in New York, I'll be sure to look you up."

The corners of her lips turned up. "You do that, cowboy."

Jared's chest tightened. He really was going to miss her.

"Goodbye, Texas," she said, a nickname she'd given him on their second date because he was so proud of the state in which he was born.

He gave her a mock salute. "Goodbye, New York," he replied and left the kitchen.

His dad and the senator were in deep conversation when Jared returned to the living room.

"I'm going home," he said, walking toward the door without pausing. "I'll be over to see you later this afternoon, Dad."

"Now wait just a minute, young man," he heard Senator Russell say as the door closed behind Jared. "Don't think you're going to get away with this kind of behavior with my daughter. You may be used to..." His voice faded away by the time Jared reached his truck.

"What a mess," Jared muttered to himself. "What possessed me to show up here last night?"

He shook his head in dismay and drove away from the Russell home.

Two

Jared walked into his house and headed into the kitchen to make coffee. He was too old for this. His body couldn't take the wear and tear of drinking too much. He'd actually never been much of a drinker. He certainly didn't miss alcohol when it wasn't available, such as in Saudi Arabia. So why had he blacked out?

Damn it! He'd gone to town last night because he'd been too tired to make himself something to eat. What had possessed him to start drinking so heavily? Seeing his old classmates again? Shooting pool? Had they switched to tequila?

He didn't have a clue.

While the coffee was brewing, he went in and took a shower and put on clean clothes. He managed to eat a couple of pieces of dry toast with his coffee. As soon as he was through eating, Jared called Matt, determined to find out what had happened.

As soon as Matt answered, Jared said, "Hey, Matt, this is Jared."

"Jared! Boy, am I glad to hear from you. Are you feeling better today?"

Cautiously, Jared said, "Why do you ask?"

"Well, you started feeling bad so suddenly, I was worried. Was Ted able to get you home all right?"

"Ted? Ted, who?"

"Boy, you must still be out of it. Ted was one of the guys shooting pool with us last night. Don't you remember?"

"I only remember being with you and Denny." When Matt didn't say anything Jared finally said, "Tell me what happened to me last night. It's important."

"Are you saying you really don't remember?" Matt asked incredulously.

"You have no idea how much I wish I did."

"Well, let's see. Do you remember shooting pool?"

"Now that I do remember," Jared said, rubbing his forehead. "If I remember correctly, at one time I was two up on you."

"That's right. Remember saying that when we finished that game, you were going home because you were tired and wanted to get some sleep?"

"Yeah…maybe…I'm not sure."

"Before we finished the last game, one of the men at the bar came over to watch us play. I've seen him in there a time or two. Always in a suit. Said he was a sales rep for a pharmaceutical company and New Eden was part of his area."

For the life of him, Jared couldn't conjure up an image of a man in a suit. "Then what happened?"

"Well, after watching us a few minutes he challenged the winner. By that time you were really rolling, not missing a shot, so no one was surprised when you won that one."

"Was I drinking a lot?"

Matt laughed. "You? Of course not, which was why you were shooting so well. I gotta admit, me and Denny had started earlier in the afternoon, so we were way ahead of you. You probably had a couple of beers. Oh, yeah, I remember now. Ted bought us all a round of drinks. That one couldn't have been more than your third one. What's the matter, guy? Can't hold your liquor like you used to?"

As Matt talked, Jared got some fragmented images. A guy in a suit, his collar open, his tie stuck halfway in his coat pocket. The problem was, he couldn't visualize the guy's face.

"I guess not," he finally replied.

"Anyway, the two of you began to play. A little later, you seemed to be having trouble focusing your eyes and you complained of feeling dizzy. You don't remember that?"

"No, I don't," he replied slowly, thinking. Was it possible this Ted character put something in his drink? He closed his eyes. A sales rep, huh. Probably had access to all kinds of drugs.

Was he being paranoid?

"Matt, did I leave by myself?"

"Hell, man, you could barely walk. You were slurring your words something pitiful and you moved like your legs were made of rubber."

"So how did I get home?" he asked, curious to know if Matt knew where he'd spent the night.

"Ted said he needed to be getting on down the road and offered to take you home. He said he knew exactly where the Crenshaw ranch was and it was on his way."

"So I agreed to leave with a stranger?"

"You weren't in any shape to agree to anything. Ted had to practically drag you out of there. So what happened after that? Did he rob you, steal the truck, leave you along the highway somewhere, what?"

"None of the above. What about my truck?"

"Yeah, that was a little puzzling, I gotta admit. When I left a little later, I looked around and your truck was gone. I began to wonder if you'd sobered up some once you got some fresh air in your lungs. I thought maybe you decided to drive yourself home. I don't mind telling you I was worried about you. I figured that, in the shape you were in, you'd be sleeping late this morning. I planned to wait until around noon to give you a call to make sure you were all right."

"I'm getting there." He paused, not wanting to arouse Matt's suspicions about where he might have spent the night. "The next time you see Ted, thank him for me and have him give you his card. I definitely owe him a drink."

Or something.

"Sure thing, although I got the impression from something he said that he doesn't come through this way very often."

Why doesn't that surprise me?

"Well, I seem to be recovering just fine this morning. Guess that'll teach me to know my limit and not drink so much from now on. It was good to see you guys last night. Maybe I'll see you again one of these days."

"Sounds good. Take care of yourself."

"Believe me, I fully intend to."

Jared arrived at his parents' home a little after two. He'd gone back to bed, slept several hours and woke up feeling much better, well enough to make himself a hearty lunch.

As soon as he stepped down from his pickup, his dad's hunting hounds—all of them eager to be the first to greet him—surrounded Jared in a joyous, baying chorus. There seemed to be at least a dozen of them milling around him until they finally settled down enough for him to count four.

Jared looked up and saw his dad watching him from the porch with his arm braced against one of the pillars. When their eyes met, Joe nodded, unsmiling. When Jared reached Joe's side, he said, "You know, Dad, I've been thinking and I'm puzzled about why you were brought into this mess. Don't you find that a little odd?"

Joe turned and walked into the house. "I'll admit I was surprised that R.W. called me. But I'll tell you this right now—he's ready to fetch his shotgun and call a preacher before the day's over."

Jared followed him into the house and looked around. "Where's Mom?"

"She and Ashley are off doing something or other, which is just as well for now."

"You didn't tell her why you were called out of bed at an ungodly hour this morning?"

Joe looked at him. "She didn't ask and I didn't volunteer any information. I see no reason to discuss the matter until something has been worked out."

"C'mon, Dad. There's nothing to work out. Yes, I definitely woke up in the wrong bed this morning. I've apologized to Lindsey. As far as I could tell she accepted my apology. She's twenty-five years old, Dad! What happened isn't any of the senator's business."

He followed his dad through the house to the back porch. "What's his problem, anyway?"

"Since I never had a daughter, I can only guess that he's being protective of her, wouldn't you say?"

Jared stared out at the vista of rolling hills. "I can understand that, but don't you think he overreacted a tad? I mean, she hadn't been raped. As a matter of fact—to clear the record here—we've never been intimate, despite what you saw this morning."

"It's a little hard for me to be sympathetic, given the circumstances. Russell is loaded for bear and he's going to make life extremely difficult for you—and the rest of the family—until you marry her."

"Something strange is going on, Dad."

"I would say more out of character, or at least different from who I thought you were until this morning."

"Say whatever you like, Dad, it doesn't matter. What does matter, to me at least, is that I found out from Matt this morning that I left the Mustang Bar last night with some guy I don't know. Think about it. Have I ever done that before?"

Joe was quiet for a few minutes. "I'll admit it doesn't sound much like you. But then again, I haven't been around you a lot since you've been working overseas so much. Have you developed a drinking problem? Maybe suffering from blackouts?"

Jared muttered obscenities beneath his breath. "No, Dad. I have an occasional beer. I couldn't have had more than three beers last night stretched out over several hours."

"You appeared to have quite a headache this morning."

Jared sat up. "Exactly. So what do you think might have caused that?"

"If not a hangover, then I have no idea."

"Well, this guy—his name is Ted—happens to work as a sales rep for a pharmaceutical company. What if he put something in my drink?"

"Now I think you're grasping at straws, son. What possible reason would the man have for doing something like that?"

Jared leaned back in his chair with a sigh. "That's what

I can't figure out. That, and how my truck and I ended up at Senator Russell's place. Matt said I became ill while I was shooting pool and this Ted guy offered me a ride home. If that's true, and I have no reason to doubt Matt, then my truck should have been at the Mustang. Only it wasn't. According to Matt, he didn't think I was capable of driving anywhere last night."

"Interesting." Joe stood. "I'm going to have some iced tea. Want some?"

"Sounds good."

"I'll be right back."

When Joe returned, he said, "So you think somebody got this Ted person to play a joke on you?"

"Hmph. Some joke. Even Lindsey said she thought it was a prank of some kind, but I believe I grew out of that stage about fifteen years ago. And why drive in the opposite direction from the ranch? I've picked up Lindsey from her home several times, but if I was in the shape Matt describes, I certainly wouldn't have been feeling amorous."

Joe's lips quirked. "Good point." They sat there in companionable silence for a while until Joe asked, "What do you intend to do?"

"I haven't the foggiest idea. Lindsey has no desire to get married anytime soon, which is fine with me. I don't know what else I can do to get the senator to calm down."

"I realize that nobody, not even the senator, can force you into a marriage you don't want. But I won't pretend that his anger at you won't spill over onto the rest of the family."

"And you think the family's going to be damaged by this?"

"Quite possibly."

"Because of the water rights thing?"

"Yes."

Jared shook his head in disgust. "This really stinks, you know, Dad? Somebody is working hard to put me between a rock and a hard place. There's not a chance in the world that Lindsey is going to marry me and yet I don't want to cause any harm to the family. I can't force her to marry me any more than the senator can." He scrubbed his face with his hands and sighed. "Do you think he'll calm down about this?"

"I doubt it."

"Even if I could convince her to change her mind, what do you think our chances of making the marriage work would be?"

"Oh, I don't know. Somewhere between slim and none, I reckon."

They sat without speaking and stared at the scenery for almost an hour before Jared spoke again.

"All right, Dad, I'll talk to her. Maybe we can work something out that will make her father happy."

"Does that mean you'll marry her?"

Jared sighed. "Yeah, if that's what it takes to get the senator off my back."

Three

Jared drove the five miles or so from his parents' home to his house wondering if he'd wake up from this nightmare anytime soon.

He was being railroaded and he knew it, but had no way to prove it at the moment.

The fact was that none of the many members of the Crenshaw clan could afford to make an enemy of Senator Robert William Russell. Access to water was a big concern to every landowner in the Southwest, especially those with large herds of livestock.

The question was whether or not the senator would be so petty as to hold Jared's behavior against his entire family. Jared didn't want to do anything to jeopardize the progress the family had made in bringing to Congress's attention the need for a review of outdated water regulations. Senator Russell knew full well his importance in the endeavor.

So what was Jared supposed to do? Go talk to the senator some more? He'd explained in every way he knew how that he hadn't intentionally chosen to sleep in Lindsey's bed. His explanations didn't appear to hold any weight with the good senator.

Let's face it—since he had no memory of last night, he couldn't convince anyone of his intentions. Sure, Lindsey really turned him on, although he couldn't begin to explain why, even to himself. Maybe it was her subtle sexiness—she didn't call attention to herself in the way she dressed. She was a class act. He knew that from the first time he'd seen her.

He went to bed that night feeling as though he were carrying the weight of the world on his shoulders. He didn't have to like the idea, but somehow he needed to convince Lindsey that marriage might be the best solution to their thorny problem.

Would marriage to Lindsey be so bad? That is, if she understood there wouldn't be a real marriage. They could agree to marry in order to pacify her father while he felt he had a duty to his family to resolve the issue.

As his dad so succinctly put it, their marriage probably wouldn't last long. But did that really matter? He was waiting for his next assignment. He'd know in a week or so where he'd be sent, most likely out of the country. They wouldn't have to live together. Well, to please the senator, they could pretend to live together. His place was large enough for both of them. It had two bedrooms with separate bathrooms.

She'd be leaving in a few weeks for New York. At least her father would have to get off her back. As a married woman, she would no longer have to answer or explain anything to her father, or anyone else.

Once he was through with his next assignment, he'd return to the States and they could get a quiet divorce, or annulment, or whatever legal procedure would sever the bonds.

He'd talk to her tomorrow—preferably without her father being present—and explain his idea in a logical and rational manner. Hopefully, she would see the benefits for both of them and would agree to go through with some quick ceremony.

He closed his eyes and, because he felt he'd found an acceptable solution to their dilemma, went to sleep.

Jared woke up early the next morning, before the sun had appeared on the horizon, and made a pot of coffee. When it was ready, he sat in one of the wooden rocking chairs on the back porch and watched the sunrise, his boot resting against the railing where he could keep a gentle motion going.

He checked his watch. He'd give her another hour before he called and, meanwhile, was content to sip coffee and watch the day begin.

When he decided it was late enough to call her, he took his cordless phone out to the porch and propped his feet on the railing with his ankles crossed.

The phone rang a couple of times before he heard the receiver being picked up. He was relieved to hear Lindsey's voice. "Hello?"

He really liked her voice—low and soothing, always gave him a peaceful feeling.

"Hi, Lindsey." He waited for her to respond and when she didn't, he added, "This is Jared Crenshaw."

"Yes?"

So she wasn't happy to hear from him. Not that he blamed her but her attitude toward him wasn't going to help him make his case. He cleared his throat.

"I'd like to see you today, if you have time."

"Why?" she asked baldly.

"I want to talk to you about some things."

"Frankly, Jared, I can't think of anything that we need to discuss. Since I was forced to listen to my father rant and rave most of yesterday because of you, I can't imagine anything you could possibly say that I would want to hear."

She was really ticked, that was for sure. "C'mon, Lindsey, give me a break. I'm not your enemy. How about cutting me a little slack and agreeing to meet me in New Eden for breakfast?"

She didn't respond.

He sighed. "Please?"

"Are you sure you're not kin to my father? Neither one of you can take no for an answer."

He laughed. "If I were, then we'd really be in big trouble, wouldn't we?"

"I'm glad you find this amusing."

"Lighten up, will you? I really need to talk to you and I'd rather do it in person."

"Oh, all right," she said ungraciously.

He released the breath he'd been holding. "Thank you," he said. "Have you ever eaten at Sally's Café on the north side of the courthouse square in New Eden?"

"No."

"It's easy to find. Why don't we meet there around nine o'clock and have breakfast together. That should give both of us enough time to drive into town."

He heard her long-suffering sigh. "I'll see you at nine."

Once he hung up, Jared smiled. He reminded himself that they knew each other. Not well, but they had built up a little history in their relationship. He doubted that she was as angry with him as she was frustrated with her father's haranguing. Since he was the subject, he could see why Lindsey wouldn't be too thrilled to see him again. But once he explained...well, at least he had a chance now to convince her that his idea would work out well for both of them.

He spotted Jake near one of the horse barns as he drove past the area, and stopped. "How's it going, bro?" he asked.

Jake walked over to the truck and leaned his elbow on the open window. He took his time noting Jared's careful grooming and grinned. "Why, hello there, stranger. Good to see you again."

Jared made a face. "Very funny. I take one day off and I catch hell from you. Considering I'm unpaid help, you could gimme a break."

"Good point," Jake said, obviously amused about something. Jared didn't have to wait long to find out why. "From what I can see, I'd say you're not dressed for work today, either."

Jared sighed. "I don't remember your being such a pain when we were kids."

"Oh, I was, believe me." They broke into laughter as they recalled some of their childhood memories.

"I need to go into town this morning," Jared finally said. "I thought I'd see if there's anything you need while I'm there."

"I ordered some things at the feed store that are probably ready to be picked up."

Jared nodded. "Will do. I should be back in an hour or so. I can put in a few hours for you today, if you need me."

Jake adjusted his hat and pulled the brim low over his eyes. "Well, if you're back in time, you might want to take a ride with me. One of the men reported seeing tire tracks in one of the canyons. Ever since the sheriff found those car thieves a few weeks ago, I've been keeping a closer eye on things around here. I don't want anybody to think they can use this land for illegal activities."

"I'd like to do that. I haven't been out on the ranch in a long time."

Jake looked stern. "I'm not taking the truck, bro. I'm riding."

"You think I can't manage to stay on a horse or something?"

Jake laughed and punched him on the shoulder. "Let's just say that it's been a while since you've spent much time on horseback and the place isn't that easy to get to from here. You'll be rubbing liniment on your butt before bedtime."

"I still have plenty of calluses from growing up around horses. I think I can handle it."

Jake nodded. "I'll see you when you get back, then."

This is awful. Lindsey stood inside her walk-in closet and surveyed its contents nervously. She wanted to appear calm and comfortable when she met Jared. All right. At least pretend to feel comfortable. She couldn't decide whether to wear slacks or a dress. If she chose a dress, which one? Or maybe a skirt would be better, something casual.

What difference does it make?

She didn't want to answer that question.

She couldn't help but wonder what might have happened if they'd been alone when they woke up yesterday morning. Of course that was nonsense. He would have been just as hungover and she would have been just as shocked. At least they wouldn't have had to deal with her father and his over-the-top reaction.

Lindsey glanced at her watch. If she didn't make up her

mind soon, she was going to be late meeting Jared. With a huff of exasperation, she closed her eyes and pulled something out of the closet.

Lindsey spotted Jared sitting in his truck as soon as she had parked near the café. He got out and opened her door before she'd finished unfastening her seat belt.

The skirt of her dress had inched up her thighs and she hastily tugged it back down.

"Good morning, ma'am," he said, drawling the words.

"Yes, it is, isn't it?" she replied politely. They turned and walked toward the café.

Once there, he opened the door for her. The aroma of coffee, cinnamon rolls and hot food engulfed them, along with the sound of many voices. The café was almost full.

"Mornin', Jared," several of the men said, although for some reason they were looking at her. She'd never been to the café before. She recognized a few of the faces she'd seen at the Crenshaw party, but wasn't surprised they didn't remember her. She generally blended into any crowd she was in.

Jared leaned toward her and said, "See those people getting up from the last booth? Let's get it before someone else decides to move over there from the counter."

He placed his hand on her waist, startling her, and followed her to the back of the café. She couldn't believe how friendly everyone was, greeting Jared as though they hadn't seen him in years.

She was glad to reach the table and to slip onto the bench seat. When she glanced at him, she was puzzled by his expression.

"Is there something wrong?" she asked.

He smiled ruefully. "Aw, it's just this town. People don't

have anything better to do with their time than to mind other people's business."

The waitress showed up to clean off the table and pour them some coffee. Once she left, Lindsay said, "I'm afraid I don't understand what you mean."

"You may have wondered why I generally took you into some of the larger towns every time we went out. That's because I didn't want to subject you to all this speculation. A few probably recognize you from the party, but every man here wants me to know he's aware I'm with a good-looking lady, just in case I missed the fact that all eyes were on you as soon as we walked through the door."

She flushed. "I just thought they were being friendly."

"Oh, they're that, all right. You just watch. Most of them will find some reason to come back here to say something to me so I can introduce you." He didn't look particularly pleased about it. He drank some coffee and then added, "Of course you're probably used to that kind of attention everywhere you go."

Lindsey had her cup halfway to her mouth when he spoke. She stared at him in surprise and carefully replaced her cup on the Formica tabletop. "You must be joking."

He crossed his arms on the table and leaned forward. "I'm dead serious. You probably cause a near riot wherever you are."

"Not so you'd notice," she replied wryly and finally tasted her coffee. "I didn't see anyone staring at me when we went to Austin that day or when we were in Fredericksburg or Kerrville."

"Then you just weren't paying attention."

Fortunately the waitress showed up at that time to take their orders, which eased Lindsey's tension somewhat until she realized she hadn't given the menu a glance. She quickly scanned it, ordered and listened in amazement at the amount of food Jared ordered.

When they were alone once again, she said, "You said you wanted to talk to me about something."

"Um, yeah. That's right."

She raised her brows and waited.

"I think I've come up with a plan that will take care of things."

"I can't imagine what that could be."

"I think we should consider getting married."

She froze and stared at him, unable to believe what she was hearing. "Absolutely not. I thought we agreed on that yesterday."

"I don't mean a real marriage."

"You want us to pretend to be married?"

"No! I mean, it will be legal and everything, but we won't tell anyone why we decided to get married. I mean, the real reason."

"Oh, you're talking about the shotgun aimed at your back?"

She was impressed that he didn't look behind him, although his shoulders twitched. He pulled at his earlobe. "I've given the matter a lot of thought and looking at it from everybody's standpoint, it seems to me that we could work something out. I mean, it wouldn't be like we'd be living together for long. You'll be going to New York, anyway, and I'll be leaving on a new assignment about the same time.

"You could stay at my house. There's an extra bedroom you can have. We get married, we work in different places. After a few months we get a divorce. Or whatever."

"Knowing how you feel about marriage," she said, "I really commend you for coming through like that. You're taking responsibility for what you did and you want to make amends."

"Then it's a go?"

"Actually, it's a no-go."

He looked at her, completely bewildered. Men. How could they be so obtuse? She leaned closer to him. "I refuse to be coerced into a marriage that neither of us wants in order to appease my father. I'm surprised you are."

"Lindsey, since we've been dating we've both ignored the fact that your father is a very powerful man. He has a lot of clout. The Crenshaws don't want to make an enemy of him."

"He's not angry at the Crenshaws, Jared. He's furious with you."

"Okay, I'll grant you that. However, I don't want him taking out his anger on my family."

He paused when the waitress appeared with their plates. For the next several minutes they made very little conversation. Lindsey watched Jared methodically put away three eggs, three pancakes, four slices of bacon and four links of sausage.

Finally, she could no longer contain herself. "Do you always eat so much for breakfast?"

He looked at her, puzzled by the question. "Well, sure. If I'd had an egg and a couple pieces of toast, like you did, I'd be hungry in an hour."

She grinned. "I can't imagine how your mother managed to feed all you guys when you were still living at home."

He shrugged. "She's always had plenty of help in the kitchen and with the household duties, but Dad used to say that we ate enough to feed a starving nation."

He smiled and she couldn't help responding. She really liked Jared. If the truth were known, she was attracted to him a little too much. It was tempting to take him up on his offer, but that was her silly emotions talking. A marriage between them wouldn't work. She'd gotten to know him well enough these past few weeks to face the reality of the situation.

She loved the East. He was pure Texan, born and bred, and wouldn't have it any other way. She was interested in art. He was interested in sports. Oh, there were hundreds of reasons why this would never work and she knew it.

"My father isn't vindictive or spiteful, Jared. He is fair in his assessments, at least as a politician. Yes, he's overprotective of me. You already know that. Once he calms down, I know he'll see reason. Just give him some time."

Jared couldn't think of anything to say that would make her change her mind. Which meant she refused to marry him. Which should be a big relief. So why was he searching for something to say to convince her she was wrong?

The waitress removed their plates and refilled their cups. When they were alone once again, he said, "I've found out more information about the other night since I talked to you yesterday."

"What more information do you need, Jared?"

"I was set up by somebody."

She frowned. "Set up? What does that mean?"

"I spoke to my friends who were shooting pool with me. They said a stranger came over to shoot some pool with us. He hadn't been there long when I suddenly became ill. According to my friends, I left the bar with some guy I've never heard of who offered me a ride home. It's quite obvious he took me to your place, instead."

"That makes no sense. Why would he do something like that?"

"I have no idea, but when I find the guy, I'm going to

get some answers from him. One of them is how he got my truck out here. My friend Matt said I was in no condition to drive, he was certain of that. I think the guy put something in my drink."

"Aren't you being a little paranoid, Jared? Maybe—for whatever reason—you told him that you lived at our place. If he was a stranger, he wouldn't know the difference."

"Well, if I was as bad off as Matt said, I would have been bumping into walls, dropping things, making a hell of a lot of noise. And I agree with you—you couldn't possibly have slept through that much commotion. So obviously, I didn't. Somebody put me to bed, Lindsey. Someone who was fairly certain that you'd sleep through the night."

"That's the most bizarre thing I've every heard of. Talk about far-fetched conspiracy theories, that one should win a prize."

He was losing his cool, which irritated him further. Why was she ignoring the obvious? He narrowed his eyes slightly. "All I know about the stranger is that his first name is Ted." He waited, but she made no comment. "Sound familiar?"

That certainly got a reaction. She stiffened. "What's going on here, Jared? First you propose and now you're implying that I—that I—what are saying? Are you suggesting that I arranged for you to be brought to my home and placed in my bed?" Her voice rose slightly at the end and he quickly looked around.

In a low voice, he replied, "Maybe not you, but somebody sure as hell did."

"*Maybe* not me?" she repeated in an icy voice.

"Well, maybe your dad had something to do with it."

"Just so you know, Jared Crenshaw," she said through clenched teeth, "my father happens to be one of the most honest, most decent, most respected men that I have ever known. And yet you've accused him of being capable of a vendetta against your family, of setting you up for some unknown reason. My father loves me and he would never do anything to embarrass or hurt me." She carefully placed her paper napkin on the table.

"If I haven't already made it clear to you, Mr. Crenshaw, you would be the very last man I would ever think of marrying. I am stunned by your boundless arrogance." She slipped off the bench and, despite her flashing eyes and obvious temper, quietly said, "If you'll excuse me."

Lindsey left the café as calmly as possible, actually smiling at a few of the people who happened to catch her eye. Inside, she was seething.

How dare he suggest that? Lindsey shook her head. She refused to think about it. He suggests marriage to her and in almost the same breath accuses her—or maybe her father—for the situation they were in.

And to think that she had actually liked him up until now! Boy, had she made a huge error in judgment. Beneath all that charm, affability and good looks was a sleazy, arrogant louse she hoped never crossed her path again.

After paying the bill, Jared walked out of the café and stood looking around the square. He thought of how disappointed in him his dad was. He thought about the good senator and the possible wrath that would soon come down on the family.

And he thought of Lindsey. He could have handled the matter more diplomatically but—damn it!—somebody knew what was behind all this.

So he'd deal with the senator and he'd figure out a way to find out something—anything—on the man named Ted.

Most important of all, he would forget he'd ever met or dated Lindsey Russell.

Four

From his position at the head of the table, Joe Crenshaw raised his glass. "I'd like to make a Thanksgiving toast," he said, "because I'm not only thankful but honored to have so many family members here to enjoy the mouth-watering meal that several of our wives have put together."

Jared said a silent amen to that one. By the time he'd tasted everything he was too full for the pies set out on the sideboard.

His dad's three brothers and their wives were here, as well as his mom's two sisters and their husbands. Most of his various cousins had made other plans and he and Jake were the only two of the brothers here.

Their Thanksgiving celebration was held at the hacienda, where there was plenty of room for everyone, and Jared was touched to see the older members get together. He hoped that someday he and his brothers would be gathered with their families in a similar scene.

Not that he expected to have a family. He enjoyed what he did. He enjoyed working around the world, looking for the almost invisible signs that oil lay beneath the land.

No wife would be interested in having a husband who was absent for months, sometimes years, at a time.

He'd gotten a call on Monday that he'd be returning to Saudi Arabia for an undetermined amount of time around the first of January. The irony didn't escape him. Had Lindsey agreed to marry him, they would have had only a few weeks to pretend they were a happy married couple—a necessity if they were to please the good senator—before they'd gone their own way.

"I also have a toast," Jake said, calling Jared away from his thoughts. "It gives me great pleasure to announce that Ashley and I are expecting an addition to the family in mid-summer."

Jared joined the family in congratulations and excited planning for an event that was at least seven or eight months away. Jared couldn't help teasing his brother a little. "Not wasting any time populating the area, are you, bro?"

Jake laughed. He and Ashley sat with Heather between them. The little girl was chattering about all sorts of ideas for a new baby, causing general laughter.

"We decided to wait a while before we told anyone."

Ashley spoke up. "That we did. He managed to keep quiet for—oh, let's see—almost seventy-two hours!"

A baby. Since Jake had been unaware that he had a daughter until this past summer, Jared knew how much Jake welcomed the opportunity to be there for the birth of the new arrival.

Joe glanced at his watch. "Well, gentlemen, are you ready to adjourn to the living room? The Cowboys' game will be starting shortly."

Gail said, "Now you know Joe's secret. The real reason we're here today is so you men can enjoy the giant-screen television Jake and Ashley just acquired!"

The scraping of chairs and general laughter that followed made Jared smile. He was grateful, very grateful, for a family like this one. Which was why he felt he'd let the family down by not resolving his issues with the Russells.

He'd talked to a couple of his uncles before dinner and they'd admitted that Senator Russell had suddenly become too busy to return their calls.

His dad had been right but Lindsey obviously saw her father through rose-colored glasses. He'd spent many sleepless nights searching for a way to undo the damage that he'd caused. It no longer mattered how or why he'd been in Lindsey's bed. The damage was done and he could think of no way to make the problem go away.

Unless he married Lindsey, of course, and that would never happen. More than once he'd thought about going over there and throwing himself on his knees before her, pleading for her to marry him.

Yep, he was losing it and that was a fact.

By the time Jared pushed back his chair and stood, the women had gathered plates and dishes and were taking them into the kitchen. He gathered up some, as well, and followed them.

"Oh, my gosh!" his aunt Colleen said, grabbing her chest. "Gail! Tell me your secret! How did you manage to train your son to help clear the table?"

Well, now he felt like a complete fool. "Just thought I'd do my part," he drawled, and winked at his mom.

She walked over and kissed his cheek. "Thank you for your good deed of the day, son. Now, go watch your ballgame."

"Everything was delicious, ladies," he said, and was rewarded by several hugs before he followed the rest of the men into the living room.

Most of the chairs and sofas were already taken, so Jared snagged a large throw pillow and stretched out on the floor. He had to admit that the large screen was truly awesome and he settled himself in to enjoy the rest of the day.

The game was a close one and the only sounds in the room were the announcer's voice and noise from the Crenshaws—cheers when the Cowboys scored and groans when the other team scored.

The Cowboys had a slight lead as the clock ticked down to the end of the second quarter and halftime.

"Unca Jared, you know what?"

Jared looked up and saw Heather beside him. He smiled at her and asked, "What, sweetheart?"

"I's going to have a baby brother or sister one of these days!"

"I *am* going to have a baby," he corrected.

"You are? Then we'll have two babies!"

The men burst into laughter. He sat up and looked at each one of them. "Not funny, guys." He looked back at Heather. "I'm not having a baby, honey. Your mommy is."

"Yes!" She clapped her hands with glee.

"I can see you're really excited."

"Uh-huh, 'cause I can teach her all kinds of things and she can wear my clothes and play with my dolls. I can hardly wait."

Jake looked over at his daughter and winked at Jared. "And if you have a brother?"

"Oh. Well. I'll just play with him, I guess. Maybe teach him stuff."

Jake laughed. "That's what we're afraid of."

Ashley walked into the room and said, "Sorry to interrupt, Jared, but you've got a phone call."

He glanced at the television screen. Only a couple of minutes left in the second quarter and the score was too close for comfort. Who would know to call him here? Then again, it was Thanksgiving, when families got together. Whoever it was could wait until the game was over. With his eyes focused on the television, he said, absently, "Maybe you could take a message for me. Do you know who it is?"

"Lindsey Russell."

Jared jumped to his feet so quickly that he almost knocked Heather over. He quickly grabbed her so she wouldn't fall. "Sorry," he muttered while the rest of the men in the room laughed.

"He's got it bad," his uncle Jeff said to the room in general. "Anytime a woman can drag him away from a close ball game, we know he's a goner!"

Jared glanced at his dad. Only the two of them knew the significance of this call. He strode to the door and down the hallway to Jake's office. Why would she be calling *him?*

He picked up the phone and gruffly said, "This is Jared."

She didn't speak right away and when she did, her voice sounded muffled. "I apologize for disturbing you today."

"No problem. What do you need?"

Another pause. "I'd like to meet with you as soon as you're available."

"Why?" he asked brusquely.

She gave a quavery laugh and that's when he realized she was crying. What was going on here?

"I deserved that, I guess. I wasn't very nice to you the last time we spoke."

"Well, yeah, that about covers it."

"I'm sorry. I really am. And I've been thinking about what you said."

"About what?"

"Our getting married."

He sank down into Jake's chair. "Oh, yeah?"

"The thing is—" She stopped and he could hear a soft sob. "I'm sorry, this is so hard." He waited and then she said, "I'm at the New Eden hospital. Dad had some kind of spell after dinner. He put it down to indigestion because he'd overeaten, but I talked him into coming to the emergency room. The doctors think it's his heart."

Jared was honestly surprised. He didn't think the man actually had a heart, as cold-blooded as he appeared to be. His only redeeming feature in Jared's mind was his love for his daughter—if love was what his possessiveness could be labeled.

"I'm sorry," he said quietly. And he was sorry that Lindsey was taking this so hard.

"I really hate discussing this over the phone. Would it be possible for you to meet me here at the hospital?"

"Now?" he asked, the ball game flashing through his mind. He also recalled that Senator Russell hadn't been taking calls from the Crenshaws. So now she wanted to discuss the possibility of marriage, which would no doubt go a long way toward appeasing the senator.

"If it isn't inconvenient for you."

He shrugged off the idea of telling her he'd be there after the game was over. "Okay. I'll leave now. Should be there in a half hour or so."

"Thank you, Jared," she quietly replied.

He could think of nothing to say to that.

"I'll see you," he said and hung up the phone.

He sat there staring at the historical map of the region that Jake had framed and placed on the wall across from his desk. The map showed the original boundaries of the Crenshaw ranch from over a hundred and fifty years ago.

His ancestors had truly had to battle to hang on to the land. They'd faced destructive weather, raiding war parties and disease in both the humans and livestock.

The map was a reminder to Jared that what he was dealing with at the moment was nothing compared to what members of his family had faced long before he was born.

He was a Crenshaw and darned proud of it. If marrying Lindsey would help to preserve what his ancestors had fought for, and from the sound of things she was reconsidering her answer, then he would marry her.

He found his mom in the sunroom with the rest of the women. "I've got to go. Please save me some of that pie, okay?"

"Of course," she said grinning. "I'll put it in your refrigerator on our way home this evening."

"Thanks." He looked at the other women. "Good to see everyone again. We should get together more often."

Ashley chuckled. "We do, Jared. You're just not around. Maybe if you'd stop spending so much time overseas, we'd get a chance to see *you* more often."

"Good point." He didn't bother telling any of the men that he was leaving, although the thought did occur to him that he could get them to tape the second half.

Naw, he could survive. This once.

The hospital, named after Jared's great-grandfather, Jonathan C. Crenshaw, had been built in the late sixties. Jon's two sons had donated the land and building to the community in his name. Newer wings had been added since then and an excellent staff worked there.

When he pulled into the parking lot, he was surprised at the number of cars there until he walked inside and saw the lobby full of people milling around. Most of them were on cell phones or held cameras. Reporters, no doubt.

Jared made his way to the information desk and in a low voice said, "I'm Jared Crenshaw. Senator Russell's daughter is expecting me."

"Oh! Yes, Mr. Crenshaw, she left a message to allow you to join her." She nodded toward one of the doors. "Go through there and you'll see signs directing you to the Intensive Cardiac Care Unit."

"Thanks."

As he pushed through the door, Jared heard several people questioning the woman, wanting to know who he was and why he'd been allowed entry. Was he family? Was he—? He didn't hear the end of the question.

He spotted Lindsey standing in the hallway with several other people. When she saw him, she quickly wiped her eyes and walked toward him.

He'd only met her six weeks ago and had seen nothing of her for the past three weeks, so why did the sight of her give him so much pleasure? She wore a bright red turtleneck sweater that enhanced her dark hair and eyes, slim black slacks and high-heeled boots. Her hair had been pulled away from her face by jeweled clips of some kind, and it fell in a cascade to her shoulders.

Damn, but she looked good. He hated to admit to himself that he'd missed seeing her.

When they grew closer to each other, he could see the redness around her eyes and nose and he had the strongest urge to fold her into his arms and comfort her.

"Thank you for coming."

Aw, to hell with it. He pulled her against him, wrapped his arms around her and silently dared her to kick up a fuss as he held her.

Instead of fighting him, she relaxed against him, gripping him around the waist as though she'd found a buoy in a stormy sea.

Her precarious control over her emotions snapped and she broke down, sobbing into his shoulder.

Jared couldn't really blame her, no matter how uncomfortable he felt. He made no effort to say anything. Instead, he gently stroked her back until her tears eventually subsided. He handed her his handkerchief and she muttered a watery, "Thanks."

Once she had a little more control, she stepped back from him. Without meeting his eyes, she said, "Sorry to rain all over you like that."

"I don't mind. How's your father?"

She gave a tiny hiccup. "According to the doctor, they have him stabilized and are busy running tests. They're considering surgery, but haven't yet made a decision."

Jared stuck his hands in his back pockets to keep from reaching for her again. She looked desolate. He knew better than most how close she was to her father.

He glanced around the hallway and into the waiting room. "Do you have any idea who these people are?"

"Most of them are here because of Dad. They're part of his Texas staff. They're doing what they can to keep the reporters at bay until someone decides what to tell them. Right now, none of us knows what to say."

"How long has he been here?"

"Maybe four hours, maybe more. We ate early because he planned to spend the afternoon on some paperwork."

"So you waited a couple of hours before you called me?"

She looked away. "That's right. I needed to think about all the ramifications if I called you."

"Such as?"

"Whether you'd bother to take my call. Whether I could actually ask you to allow me to change my answer about our marriage. Lots of things."

There it was—the *M* word coming out of her mouth. Prepared or not, he'd tensed at the sound of it.

He cleared his throat. "Why don't we go to the cafeteria and get some coffee? We'll have more privacy there."

"All right. Let me tell one of the nurses where they can reach me."

Once again she looked regal and in control of herself walking away from him—her back straight, shoulders back, ready to deal with the world again. Her clinging to him the way she had really surprised him. He had a strong hunch she seldom allowed herself to show any vulnerability.

When she returned, they were quiet while they waited for an elevator, while they rode down and while they stood in line for some coffee. He spotted a small table in a corner of the room and nodded toward it, then followed her.

Once seated, he waited for her to say something.

"My dad has been under a great deal of stress lately and I know that what happened with us hasn't helped the situation any. I've thought about our conversation that day at the café and I believe it might work for us to get married."

"Okay."

"I mean, we're the only ones who would know that it isn't a real marriage. We can pretend to be in love…pretend to want to get married."

"It will probably relieve your mind to know that I'm going back to Saudi Arabia in January."

"Oh. Well, then, all we have to do is to get through the next four or five weeks."

"When do you want to do this?"

She glanced down at her clasped hands. Neither one of them had touched their coffee. "The sooner the better, I guess. I'm hoping that Dad's mind will be relieved. By the time we have the marriage annulled, I'm hoping he will have gotten used to the fact that I have a life away from him."

He lifted a brow. "Whatever you think. You know him better than I do."

She reached for his hand, hesitated, then placed her fingers against the back of his. "I know you don't have a very good impression of him, but he really is a wonderful man. Once you get to know him better, you'll see. He was just upset that morning..." She let the sentence dwindle away.

"Upset is a nice way of putting it. So you think if we get married, he'll rest easier."

She nodded. "Yes, I do."

"I don't know if the courthouse will be open tomorrow because of the holiday weekend. So why don't we plan to get a license Monday, find someone in the courthouse to marry us and get the deed done."

"You make it sound like we're planning to have root canals."

He withdrew his hand. "What do you want from me, Lindsey? I asked you to marry me. You've just said yes. Are you saying you want some big splashy wedding to make it look more romantic?"

He really dreaded hearing her answer because that's exactly what most women wanted. Even if he loved her, he'd hate going through all that.

"No! Of course not. But if we're going to pretend we're

eager to marry, we'll have to show some enthusiasm about it, don't you think?"

"What could be more enthusiastic than rushing into marriage as though we can't wait to get our hands on each other?"

She blushed. Ah, hell. Now he'd gone and done it.

"Look, I'm sorry. I'm just a little edgy, okay? We'll do whatever you want and I'll make certain everyone thinks we're truly happy with each other."

"I think you're right. We'll get married Monday," she said, straightening away from him. "It's the fact that we'll be married that's important."

She glanced at her watch. "Would you mind going with me to see Dad so we can tell him?"

He stood in answer. "Will they let us see him? I thought they were really strict about letting visitors in."

"I don't know. Maybe if I explain that we have news he'll be happy to hear, they'll let us slip in for a couple of minutes."

Whatever. He'd stepped onto this train and it was already gaining momentum. He'd just have to get used to it.

Once they reached the ICU again, Lindsey found her father's doctor and quickly explained what was going on. The doctor smiled, looked over at Jared who waited a few feet away, winked and said, "Hearing your news might be the best medicine we could give him. However, you'll have to make a quick announcement because I can only give you a couple of minutes with him."

The doctor opened the door and motioned them inside. The blinds were open at the large window facing the nurses' station, but at least no one could hear them. They just watched his monitors from where they sat.

Jared took Lindsey's hand and walked over to the bed.

Senator Russell certainly looked like a sick man to him. He was hooked up to all kinds of monitors and oxygen and his face was paper white and drawn.

"Dad?" Lindsey said softly.

Russell's eyes opened and slowly focused. He looked astonished to find Jared standing there.

"I won't keep you, Senator Russell," Jared said. "I just want you to know that I've finally managed to convince Lindsey to marry me. The only thing I want is your permission." He thought that last bit sounded good.

Russell looked at his daughter. "Is that true?"

"Absolutely. We're eager to get married as soon as possible. I want you to hurry up and get well, now, you hear me?"

"But…you said…moving to New York."

Jared wrapped his arm around her shoulders. "We'll deal with all of that, sir. No need for you to worry about a thing. We just want you to get back on your feet."

A nurse peeked around the door. "Time's up," she said.

Good. Jared had done all he could for his co-conspirator.

Lindsey kissed her father on the cheek and Jared followed her out of the room.

Once back at the waiting room, he asked, "What's next?"

She smiled wearily. "Your job is done for the day. If Dad has to have surgery, I want to wait until he's out of the woods before we get the license."

"And if he doesn't have surgery?"

"We'll do it Monday." She went up on tiptoe and kissed him, but before he could recover from the unexpectedness of it, she stepped back. "You're a good man, Jared Crenshaw, despite the fact that you believe in conspiracy theories. Take care," she said and walked away.

As soon as he stepped through the doors to the lobby, flashbulbs went off in his face. What the—?

"Mr. Crenshaw? Are you any kin to United States House Representative, Jed Crenshaw?"

What kind of question is that? "He's my cousin. If you'll excuse me, I'd like to—"

"Mr. Crenshaw, what is your relationship to Senator Russell?"

He continued to push his way through the group of rude reporters. When he reached the door to the outside, he turned and said, "You know, if I thought it was anybody's business I might tell you."

He strode rapidly to his truck, got in and drove off.

Five

"You're going to do what?" Janeen shouted over the phone. "Are you out of your mind? What about moving *here?* And your job? What were you thinking? Are you pregnant? That must be it. You're pregnant. Good grief, how could you—"

"Whoa, wait a minute," Lindsey replied. She had been dreading this phone call because she knew her decision was going to be difficult to explain. She'd gone to her room and closed the door in order not to disturb her father, who was resting in his bedroom at the end of the hall. "You're not giving me a chance to answer your questions, and *your* answers are off the wall. Calm down a little and I'll tell you what's happened."

"I'm calm."

Lindsey chuckled. "Sure you are. I'm sorry I haven't been in closer touch with you the past couple of weeks. A lot has been happening here."

"I should guess so." Janeen sniffed indignantly.

Lindsey took the cordless phone and climbed into the middle of her bed. She might as well get comfortable. "First of all, I'm not pregnant. I couldn't be pregnant because I've never been intimate with Jared."

"Jared? Isn't he the guy you've been seeing for—what—maybe a month?" Before Lindsey could respond, Janeen continued. "I'm gravely concerned about your state of mind, Lindsey. Getting married to a man you barely know? This doesn't sound like my sane and sensible friend."

"Now *that* we can agree on, I have to admit. There's nothing sane—or rational—about any of the things that have happened. To answer your question, yes, I've dated him a few times. We had fun together. He's a very charming guy and I really like him. However, neither one of us is looking for a serious relationship."

"Honey, getting married isn't the best way to avoid a serious relationship. You should both be running for the hills about now."

Here came the sticky part, the part she hadn't told Janeen about in hopes it would have all blown over before Lindsey moved up there.

"Then, uh, well...Dad found us in bed together." She paused, waiting for another explosion, only it didn't happen. Janeen's mild response surprised her.

"Oops."

"Oh, yes, definitely an oops." She smiled. Janeen really *was* a good friend. "Of course he thought we'd slept together—well, actually, we *did* sleep together, but neither one of us knew the other one was there in the bed."

"Lindsey, honey, I think the stress and strain of this move and the anticipation of working at the museum has been a little too much for you. And I understand, I really do. But how in the world could you end up sleeping with a guy you didn't know was there?"

"It's a mystery."

They both burst into hysterical laughter. Finally, Janeen said, "So you've decided to marry him because you slept with him?"

"Exactly."

"What century are you living in?"

"Well, it's not going to be a real marriage. Dad's been quite upset because he doesn't believe us when we attempt to explain what we don't understand ourselves. I've done my best to convince him that nothing ever happened between us, but he refuses to believe me."

"Guess that one would be a little hard to swallow, given the fact he actually *saw* the two of you."

"There is that. For a while, I thought he planned to polish up his shotgun and go hunt down Jared. Instead, he brooded. And brooded. But that's beside the point. Jared and I eventually talked over the situation and we decided the best thing for us to do was to get married. He already knows I'm moving to New York and that's fine with him. He works for one of those big oil companies with interests all around the world and he's going to Saudi Arabia about the same time as I'm moving, so, you see, the situation works out great."

"Great," Janeen slowly repeated, sounding thoughtful. "Maybe I'm slow, but frankly, I don't get it. What's the point of getting married at all if you're going to be halfway around the world from each other?"

"I told you. It isn't going to be a real marriage. We'll have the marriage annulled as soon as he returns, which could be several months to a year from now."

"And you're okay with this?"

"Yes, I am. Dad had a mild heart attack on Thanksgiving. They kept him at the hospital for a couple of days, ran a bunch of tests and sent him home, telling him to take it easy, cut out the stress in his life, or he'd end up back in the hospital with more damage to his heart."

"Ah. The light dawns. You decided to get married only after your father had his heart attack. In other words, you're doing this to keep your dad happy."

"That's it in a nutshell."

"And Jared is willing to go along with all this?"

"Yes. In fact, he asked me a few weeks ago but, at the time, I didn't believe the situation was so serious and I told him no. Obviously, I've changed my mind."

"Lindsey, Lindsey, Lindsey. I thought you were past catering to your dad. I thought you were setting boundaries, taking stands, growing independent from him."

"I am and I did. Take stands, I mean. He was determined to stop me from going to New York but I'm still going."

"Really? Did he pay Jared to slip into your bed?"

"Of course not, although Jared seems to think my dad had something to do with it."

"Intelligent man."

"What is it with you guys? Why would you think my dad would stoop to something so underhanded?"

"Because he's manipulative, for one thing. For another, he's managed to keep you under his thumb all of your life and he doesn't like to lose."

"Uh, Janeen, Jared and I getting married certainly isn't keeping me under Dad's thumb."

"True, unless it prevents you from moving. Have you told him those plans haven't changed?"

"No."

"I rest my case."

"Actually, Jared and I are having dinner with his parents and his brother and sister-in-law tomorrow. That's when we plan to tell them we're getting married because right now no one knows other than my dad. And now you."

"What do you think they'll say?"

"I have no idea. But they're very nice people, warm-hearted, friendly. I don't think they'll try to talk us out of it."

"Will they know it's all pretense?"

"No. We're keeping that part to ourselves."

"Hmm. So, do you want me to come down for the wedding?"

"We're just going to the courthouse and have a judge marry us. No need to spend your money for that."

"Aw, Lindsey, I really am sorry all this is happening to you."

Lindsey looked at the phone in surprise. She put it back to her ear. "I don't know what you're talking about."

"A marriage is something sacred, not to be taken lightly. You'll be exchanging vows you have no intention of keeping."

"We've talked about that, too, which is why we want to just go and do it in the courthouse. Someday I'll have the wedding of my dreams with the right man for me. Just as someday Jared will find the woman he can't live without." Why did the thought of that make her feel uncomfortable? "It will be as if this marriage never existed."

"Well, I know I'll never talk you out of this crazy idea once you've got your mind set. That's something I've never understood about you, Lindsey. You're tenacious, in a very ladylike way, of course, and at times downright stubborn—with everyone but your father. Dealing with him turns you into a complete wimp."

"Well, the wimp is growing a backbone where he's concerned. But then, I probably wouldn't have reconsidered the idea of marriage if he hadn't had his heart attack."

"Ha. Probably faked that."

"Janeen!"

"Okay, okay. Maybe the man is the saint you think he is. I've been wrong about people before." They were quiet for a moment before she asked, "How does Jared feel about him?"

"Lukewarm would be my guess."

"Hmm. So when are you coming up here?"

"The first week in January. I start at the museum on the seventh."

"I can hardly wait for you to get here. Your bedroom is emptied out and waiting for you. Then you can fill me in on the details of this fake marriage of yours."

Jared picked up Lindsey the next afternoon. She met him at the door and slipped outside before he could knock. "Dad's asleep and I didn't want to disturb him. The housekeeper is here in case he needs anything, and she has my cell phone number if a problem develops."

He'd picked her up in a low-slung, bright red, two-seater sports car. "Wow," she said as they walked toward it. "Where did you get that?"

He opened the door and helped her inside. "Actually, I've had it a while. I bought it about four months before I went overseas last time. Dad and Jake take it out for a spin to keep it running okay." He laughed. "Dad said it was a sacrifice of his time but he'd force himself."

She laughed.

As he backed out and turned around in the driveway, he said, "It's good to hear you laugh again."

She settled into her seat. "It feels good to find something to laugh about." She glanced at him and then away. "I appreciate the fact that you're willing to make your own sacrifice by getting married," she said lightly.

He didn't smile. "Don't mention it."

He sounded serious and she decided to drop the subject. "Have you talked to your parents?"

"You mean, since Thanksgiving?"

"Yes."

"Of course. I generally talk to them every day or two."

"Aren't they going to be surprised when they hear our plans?"

"Mother, Jake and Ashley will be, I'm fairly sure. Dad won't be."

"Oh. Of course."

Jared reached over and turned on the CD player and the music filled the car until they reached the ranch.

Lindsey hadn't seen where Joe and Gail lived until she and Jared parked in their driveway. She was surprised to find that their house was contemporary. For some reason, she'd expected to find a smaller home that looked like the hacienda.

"What a beautiful place," she said when he helped her out of the car.

"Yeah. They really are enjoying it. They've been in it for about ten years now. Mom told the architect what she wanted. Dad didn't care as long as she was happy with it."

The front door opened just as they reached the top step of the porch. "I'm glad you were able to come visit with us, Lindsey," he said. "I believe you already know Gail. Did you meet Jake and Ashley at their reception?"

"I saw you, of course," she said to them, "but we weren't introduced."

Jake grinned. "That's because my brother monopolized your time while you were there."

"My name is Heather Crenshaw."

Lindsey looked at the little girl standing between her father's boots. "I'm pleased to meet you."

"I'm four."

"Well, you're practically all grown up, aren't you?"

"I'm going to have a baby sister or brother."

Jake laughed. "Well, now that you know all our family secrets, Lindsey, why don't we all sit down."

"Dinner's almost ready," Gail said. "Heather, be sure to go wash your hands."

"Yes, ma'am," the little girl replied and scampered off.

An awkward silence fell and Lindsey didn't know how to get past it. She looked at Jared, who'd come in behind her, and he must have seen the plea for help in her eyes.

He stepped closer and put his arm around her waist. "Actually, there's another family secret I want to share with you. Lindsey and I are getting married."

Everybody but Joe stared at him as if he'd just thrown a hand grenade at them. Lindsey saw Jared and his father exchange looks and then Jared gave his dad a slight nod.

"Well!" Joe said, clapping his hands together. "This calls for a celebration. Congratulations, you two!"

Gail was the first to recover. "Oh, by all means! Let me put dinner on the table. Joe, maybe you could find some wine for toasts."

Jake stepped forward and took Lindsey's hand. "You're a brave woman, Lindsey, to take on the chore of raising this guy. I can only offer my very best wishes."

Ashley quickly followed him. "This is so exciting. Why, it's only been a couple of months since Jared insisted that he would never—" She gave a quick cough. "That is, I'm so pleased to welcome you to the family. I guess you'll be moving to the ranch soon."

"Dinner's on the table," Gail called, and they walked into the lovely, open dining room with large picture windows on two sides. Jared slipped his hand down to Lindsey's. Only then did she realize she was shaking. This was worse than awful. The Crenshaws were wonderful people and she and Jared were lying to them, making them think that—well, that they were in love and eager to get married.

And they weren't.

Jared leaned down slightly and whispered in her ear. "Relax. We've told them. No reason to be nervous now."

As the meal progressed, Lindsey slowly relaxed. Conversation covered general topics. She didn't say much, if anything, but enjoyed listening to the three men talk together, kid each other, and she knew that this was what she had missed growing up as an only child.

Everything went well until they were enjoying dessert and coffee and Gail brought up their impending marriage.

Heather looked up. "Who's getting married?"

Lindsey recalled that Heather hadn't been in the room when Jared told them. She glanced at Jared, who smiled at his niece. "Actually, Lindsey and I are getting married."

"See there, Unca Jared? See there? You are *too* going to have a baby," Heather said. Lindsey froze. "Daddy and Mommy got married and now they're going to have a baby."

Jared reached for Lindsey's hand and gently squeezed it. "That's not going to happen for us anytime soon, sweetheart."

"I am so excited," Gail said with glee, after Joe and Jake had toasted the happy couple. Lindsey's nerves tightened. She felt as though she were in a nightmare she couldn't escape. "Another wedding in the family," Gail continued. "I can hardly wait." She smiled at them. Have you picked a date, yet?"

Jared cleared his throat. "Yes, we have. We're going to

get the license tomorrow and get married while we're there."

Jared watched his mother and Ashley erupt into what he considered to be clamoring hysteria at the idea that they would consider such a thing. They must think he was a teenager planning to elope without permission.

"Jared Crenshaw," Gail said firmly, "you were not raised to behave in such a way. You are not being fair to Lindsey."

"Oh," Lindsey said, "that's all ri—"

"Neither one of us wants to make a fuss," Jared replied firmly.

Jake spoke up in a drawl, "Nice try, bro. But it's not going to fly. You might as well give up now."

Joe remained silent, watching the scene from the sidelines and occasionally glancing at Lindsey.

When she caught his gaze, Lindsey said, "We want to get married before the Christmas holidays. I don't want to make too much of it because of Dad's health."

"I can understand that," Gail said, and Lindsey sighed with relief until Gail continued. "You won't have to worry about a thing. Ashley and I can put together whatever's necessary and your dad won't have to be involved, except to give you away, of course." She looked at Ashley. "We can do a small wedding, don't you think?"

Ashley couldn't hide her amusement. "Absolutely."

"Mom," Jared began.

"Give it up, son. Your mother's right, you know. That's no way to begin a marriage." Joe's gaze was steady.

Gail got a calendar and said, "How about a week from Saturday? That will give your dad time to feel a little stronger. What do you think?"

Lindsey stared at Jared in a panic. *Say something! Do something! We can't—*

Ashley reached for Lindsey's hand, causing Lindsey to start in surprise. "Please let us do this for you, Lindsey."

Jake leaned over to Jared and murmured just loud enough for Lindsey to hear, "You might as well surrender now, you know. Saves time and believe me, this is one argument you two aren't going to win."

Jared looked at Lindsey. "What do you think?"

He gave nothing of his thoughts away. But a picture was forming in Lindsey's mind, one that embarrassed her beyond belief. They'd met six weeks ago at Jake and Ashley's wedding. Now Ashley was pregnant. Did the family think that she'd gotten pregnant, too? It didn't bear thinking about. They must think she'd trapped him into marriage, just as he'd implied she had. It would do no good at this point to attempt to explain the truth.

She forced a smile on her face and said, "I would be honored to have you help us plan a wedding to be held in not quite two weeks."

Six

"I now pronounce you husband and wife," the minister said. "You may kiss the bride."

Those were the words that sealed his fate. He was now a married man. He waited to hear a clanging in his head of cell doors being slammed shut. Instead, all he heard was the sudden silence from the gajillion people that had been delighted to accept an invitation to their sudden wedding.

He turned to Lindsey, who was watching him with a hint of wariness. Yeah, well, all of this was new to him, too. He winked at her, causing her to smile.

The kiss was an expected part of the ritual and it wasn't as if they'd never kissed before. He relaxed and put his arms around her, pulling her into his embrace, accompanied by the oohs and aahs of the sentimental women in the audience.

She lifted her mouth to his and he brushed his lips

against hers. That was all that was necessary, so why didn't he let her go instead of deepening the kiss in a possessive gesture that startled even him and caused a ripple of laughter among the guests?

The amusement stopped him. He stepped away from her and took her hand before they turned to greet their guests.

Everyone applauded. Jake, who had served as Jared's best man, clapped him on the back and said, "Congratulations, you managed to survive the ceremony."

Not funny. He acknowledged the comment with a nod and wrapped his arm around Lindsey's waist as people moved toward them.

The ceremony had been held on the large back lawn at the hacienda. Jared had to admit that the family had done a miraculous job of pulling this together so quickly.

Luckily, the weather had turned nice—cool but sunny and no wind. His mother, bless her heart, had hired a crew to set up a large tent that covered the hundreds of chairs and the altar, just in case of rain.

The smell of barbecue wafted across the area, making his mouth water. Who would have thought when he attended Jake's wedding that he'd be the next one getting married? Certainly not him.

Fresh flowers sat in large vases on each end of the table that had been used as an altar, and the air was redolent with their scent, as well. Gail's pastor officiated at the ceremony and everything had turned out just as they'd planned.

Lindsey quivered to see the horde of people coming up to greet them. She didn't know half of them, even though she knew many had flown in from Washington to attend the senator's daughter's wedding.

She'd called Janeen back to tell her of the change of plans. As she expected, her friend was pleased but decided not to come down there since Lindsey would be in New York in two or three weeks.

Therefore, Lindsey had asked Ashley to be her matron of honor. The look of joy on Ashley's face told her she'd done the right thing.

She looked over and saw her father standing beside Jared's dad just a few feet away. She couldn't remember a time when she'd seen him so happy…at least not since her mother had died.

Lindsey was thankful that his health had improved enough for him to walk her down the aisle.

Today had been the first time she'd seen Jared wearing anything other than his usual boots, jeans and a Western-style shirt. Today he wore a dark suit and tie with black dress boots, of course. She had to admit that he looked quite handsome, the dark colors emphasizing his blond, blue-eyed looks.

When she'd walked out of the hacienda this morning, her hand resting on her father's arm, and saw Jared waiting with Jake near the pastor, Lindsey had fought to keep her composure.

Although Jake and Jared were very similar in both their coloring and build, it was Jared who continued to cause her heart to race.

Jared.

Her husband.

"Have I told you that you look like a queen in your wedding gown," Jared said quietly.

"Thank you." Gail and Ashley had helped her choose a gown. She had wanted something simple and understated and she'd found the perfect one—a long-sleeved gown with a cowl neck that had a Renaissance look about it. She had ended up having the kind of wedding she'd dreamed about—and it was all a sham.

"Are you okay?" he asked.

"A little tired." Jared had been the perfect fiancé and groom, accepting all the teasing with humor and grace. No one could have guessed that he wasn't a besotted bridegroom. The kiss at the altar had probably been meant to convince everyone. If she hadn't known better, she would have been convinced that he couldn't wait to get her alone and out of that dress!

She shivered at the thought.

"Is it too cold for you to stay outside?"

"Oh, no. Once we're out in the sun I'll be fine."

Before they could leave, the photographer had to take pictures of everyone in the wedding party, the parents as well as one of the bride and groom alone.

The hours sped by until only the senator, Jared's parents, Jake and Ashley and the newlyweds were left. Everything had been carted away from the lawn and there was no sign left that there had been a wedding held there that day. The flowers were now in the house, giving off their soft scents as a reminder.

Even Heather had fallen asleep without a fuss after all the excitement of the day.

Senator Russell said, "I want to thank each of you for your handling of the wedding details and making Lindsey's day so perfect. Since y'all have done so much for the couple, I decided I would do my part by helping with the honeymoon."

Jared looked at Lindsey with a slight frown. She shrugged, having no idea what her father was up to now.

"Senator," Jared said politely, "that's really generous of you, but we decided not to go on a honeymoon just yet."

The senator laughed. "Well, now you are! We've been plotting a little behind your back. I hope you like our little surprise." He reached into his breast pocket and pulled out a fat envelope. "Here you go."

Jared handed the envelope to Lindsey. Her hands shook and he helped her open it.

Airline tickets and several brochures spilled out. "Cancun?" Lindsey asked, wondering if this day could possibly get worse. "You're sending us to Cancun?"

The senator beamed. "That's right. An all-expense-paid trip. Nothing's too good for my little girl. Now I want you to go and enjoy yourselves, explore the area, see the sights, spend some time together…just the two of you."

"You said, 'we' have been plotting. Who do you mean?"

Gail spoke up. "Actually, Ashley and I were in on this. When the senator told us what he wanted to do, we agreed to go shopping for the two of you, so you'd have the proper attire for a week in the tropics."

Lindsey didn't dare faint—they'd immediately believe that *she* was pregnant.

"How, uh, what an unexpected—it's such a surprise. Right, Jared?"

She saw a tic along his jaw. Otherwise, he looked perfectly relaxed.

"I must say, Senator Russell, you've managed to think of everything, haven't you?" There was a slight edge to his voice.

Lindsey glanced at Joe and saw that he and Jared were in silent communication.

Gail said, "Why don't you two get changed? You still have to be on the road for a while."

Jared reached for the tickets and looked at them. "These tickets say we leave out of Austin tomorrow morning at six o'clock."

"That's right," the senator said. "I've arranged for you

to stay at one of the hotels near the airport tonight. You should arrive in Cancun around one o'clock tomorrow and have plenty of time to see the place in daylight."

Jared took Lindsey's hand. "Are you up for this?" he asked, ignoring the rest of them.

What could she say? No, I'd rather keep to our plans of my moving into your place until after New Year's?

She summoned her best smile and said, "Sounds like fun, doesn't it?" without looking at him. She walked to her father and hugged him. "You're the best father in all the world. I love you, Dad." She closed her eyes and laid her cheek on his chest.

He patted her back a little awkwardly. "Good, good. I love you, too."

"Then we'd better go get changed," Jared said matter-of-factly. "We still have a two-hour drive ahead of us and it's already getting late."

"Good idea." She could put on the clothes she'd worn this morning as well as grab a few minutes alone to face this unexpected development in their plans. She took her time slipping out of her gown. She carefully hung it in the closet of the bedroom where she was changing and removed the dress she'd worn from another hanger.

She and Jared hadn't planned on this. In fact, the subject of a honeymoon had never been brought up. They had spent the last few days moving her things to his place and getting her bedroom ready for occupation for the necessary few weeks. They'd fallen into a comfortable camaraderie during the past two weeks, almost like the one they'd had when they were seeing each other.

Except for one thing—they avoided intimate contact.

And now they were going to be alone for a week in a romantic tropical paradise.

Maybe she should pack several books to read.

* * *

Jared stood staring into the closet of the bedroom where he'd grown up. He'd removed his suit, tie and dress shirt. He'd put on his customary shirt and jeans, pulled on his boots and yet he still stood there, wondering what the hell he was going to do now.

He seemed to stay in a half-aroused state whenever he was around Lindsey. He couldn't remember the last time he'd been with a woman, but he knew it had been too long for him to be able to spend a week alone with Lindsey without doing his damndest to get her into bed with him.

Which was what had gotten him into this predicament in the first place.

He'd recognized that there was no way they were going to get around this offer without seeming churlish and ill-mannered. Everybody at the wedding and reception—everybody but his dad, that is—was convinced they were madly in love with each other. Love at first sight. A race to the altar so that they could be together.

And there wasn't a thing he could do to change that.

He sincerely hoped that the good senator would suddenly find himself available to take calls from the Crenshaws.

Jared was waiting for Lindsey when she came downstairs, standing with his hands tucked into the back pockets of his jeans and rocking slowly back and forth from heel to toe in his boots.

She had her coat draped across her arm.

"I'm ready whenever you are," she said and Jared turned and saw her. "Oh. Good. That's good. Our bags are already in the car."

Her dad hugged her tightly against him. "I want you to

rest and relax this week, sweetheart. You've been a little tense lately, what with all your wedding plans and all."

"I'm sure I will," she replied, knowing she was lying.

Russell shook Jared's hand. "You take care of my girl, you hear?"

Jared looked at him with a steady gaze. "You know I will."

While Ashley and Gail hugged Lindsey, Joe pulled Jared aside. "I want you to know how proud I am of you. The rest of the family will never know what you've done to ease a delicate situation."

Jared shrugged. "Since I was the one who set the whole thing off, I figure I needed to do what I could to repair the damage I'd caused."

"Like I said. I'm prouder of you than I can possibly say."

Jared glanced at his watch. "We need to go," he said, acknowledging his father's words with a brief nod. "Ready?" he asked Lindsey with a smile.

"Oh, yes. My face hurts from having to smile so much," she said, too low for the others to hear her.

He burst into laughter, causing everyone watching them to conclude that this was the beginning of a wonderful life together.

If they only knew.

Seven

"I can't believe we're going on a honeymoon."

Jared glanced at Lindsey, who had been quiet for the hour they'd been on the road. "I'm having trouble adjusting to the idea, myself," he replied.

"We had everything worked out. We'd get married—"

"—at the courthouse—"

"—right, at the courthouse. I'd move into your house for a few weeks and then we'd go our own way."

"So we had a fancier wedding than we'd planned and now we have a surprise honeymoon. We'll have to deal with it."

"I know."

She said nothing more but Jared knew she was thinking about their first night together. Instead of separate rooms, they'd be sharing one. He'd been dwelling on the same thought and decided this was part of his continued punishment for having the audacity to sleep with the senator's daughter.

He knew he wasn't being fair. The senator wanted his daughter to have happy memories of her wedding and honeymoon. The problem was, they hadn't discussed the conditions of the marriage.

They'd agreed that after they married they would have separate bedrooms. That was clear enough. No sex. He could handle that—if she slept clear across the house from him.

Sure, he'd been in bed with her once, but he'd been unconscious at the time.

"So what are we going to do?" he asked out loud, following his train of thought.

"About what?" she asked, sounding puzzled.

Might as well get the subject out in the open. "The rules for the next week."

"I'm sorry. I was dozing and must not be fully awake. I'm afraid I'm not following you."

"I'm talking about sex," he said, his jaw clenched.

"Oh."

"Yeah."

She didn't speak right away, which meant she was thinking about possible rules. So he waited. Finally, she said, "Making love will complicate things."

"Probably."

"I mean, we made the arrangement thinking that—"

"I know what we were thinking, Lindsey. However, I'm not superhuman, nor am I immune to you. I'm a normal male with normal needs. We were together enough for you to know that you turn me on. Always have."

"Oh."

"Is that all you can say?"

"So you want to make love to me?"

"C'mon, Lindsey. You're not naive. At least, not *that* naive."

"No, I'm not. However, I'm observant. You haven't kissed me since we agreed on this until the kiss at the altar today. I decided that was because you weren't attracted to me."

"You're wrong. You have no idea how wrong. How many men have you gone out with, anyway?"

"Are you deliberately being insulting?"

"No."

"Am I supposed to ask you how many women you've been with?"

"You're missing the point here. You don't seem to know much about the male psyche. Most men want to have sex with an attractive woman. The longer he goes out with her—generally speaking, of course—the more intensely he wants to make love to her."

"Generally speaking, as you say. Well, I've never had to fight off any of the men I've dated, so I think your theory needs a little work."

"We don't attack the woman! Good grief. But we let her know in more subtle ways that we want to take her to bed."

"Crawling into my bed wasn't exactly subtle, Jared."

He felt like beating his head against the steering wheel. "I refuse to discuss that incident any further. We each have our own view of what happened, let's just leave it that way. Just so you know, I had no intention of making love to you while we were seeing each other. Because sometimes sex *does* complicate things."

"Only sometimes?"

"Okay, most of the time. Is that better? And you're just not the love-'em-and-leave-'em kind of woman."

"In other words, I'm really not your style."

"Stop putting words into my mouth."

She clapped her hands together and said, "Oh, goody! We're having our very first fight. And we've been married about—" she glanced at her watch "—almost eight, no, make that nine hours. Some kind of record, I bet."

"Very funny. Let me put it this way. Most men expect to make love to their wives on their wedding night. This is our wedding night. So—what do you say? Shall we follow tradition?"

Well, that certainly shut her up. She didn't say another word until they reached Austin and she spotted the hotel where they'd be staying.

"There it is," she said quietly, and he flipped on his turn signal.

The hotel the senator—or more likely a member of his staff—had chosen was upscale. Nothing but the best for his daughter. Once Jared checked them in and received the key card, he returned to the car with one of the hotel attendants who took their bags. He then moved the car from the entrance of the hotel and parked. "Ready?" he asked, opening his door.

He walked around and opened hers. He offered his hand, which she graciously accepted. She looked at him and said coolly, "To sleep, yes. To make love, no."

"Wow. It only took you the better part of an hour to come to that decision."

They went inside the hotel and walked to the elevator. Once the door closed, giving them privacy, she looked at him and asked politely, "Why are you being so obnoxious?"

He glanced at her and said, "Well, let me count the reasons. I'm frustrated, aroused, feeling trapped and I'm forced to spend a week pretending to be a lovesick bridegroom while keeping a careful distance from my deliciously sexy bride. I can look all I want but I can't touch."

He shrugged. "Other than that, I guess I'm just naturally obnoxious."

He was being a jerk and he knew it. The problem was, he didn't care. The past two weeks had been the toughest he'd ever spent. He'd worked hard to convince his family that marrying Lindsey was what he wanted more than anything, and he hated lying to them.

In addition, a marriage in name only didn't appeal to him in the least.

Today had been particularly harrowing. As soon as he'd seen Lindsey walking toward him in that regal gown, all he could think about was sweeping her into his arms and rushing her to the first available bed he could find where he'd keep her for at least a week.

And guess what? Her dear father made sure he'd have that opportunity!

Their luggage was already there when they arrived at their room. Jared closed the door behind them and set the lock before following Lindsey into the bedroom area. The room contained two queen-size beds separated by a bedside table. There was also a large dresser, a television cabinet, a small round table and a couple of chairs. Regardless of what else had been placed in the room, the beds dominated.

He averted his eyes while he placed her suitcase on the luggage rack that had been provided. "There you go," he said and, without looking at her, wandered over to the window. "I don't know about you," he said without turning around, "but I'm hungry. I think I'll order something from room service. Do you want anything?"

When she didn't answer, he turned and looked at her. She sat at the end of one of the beds gazing around the room as though she'd never been in a hotel room before tonight.

"Lindsey?"

"Oh! Sorry. Yes, please. A chef salad and iced tea, please."

He called in their order. When he hung up, Lindsey said, "If you'll excuse me, I'm going to take a shower."

Jared stretched out on the other bed and propped pillows behind his head. "Fine. You do that." He did his best not to think of her standing under the shower, the water trickling down her bare body, sliding between her breasts and—

She made a startled sound and he opened his eyes. Lindsey stood in front of her open suitcase with her back to him.

"What's wrong?"

She turned and looked at him with dismay. "Do you remember the old joke that goes, 'Cheer up, things could be worse, so I cheered up and sure enough things got worse'?"

"Maybe. So what's wrong now?"

"My suitcase appears to be filled with somebody else's clothes."

He walked over and peered into her bag. He picked up a few of the things and looked at them. The suitcase was filled with a rainbow of colors. Definitely tropical attire—if she wanted a good tan over a majority of her body!

"What's this?" He lifted out a peach-colored wisp of material with a bunch of lace on it.

"A nightgown," she said. Her voice quivered slightly. Was she going to cry?

He glanced at her and saw that she was nibbling her bottom lip. He thought about offering to nibble for her but figured she wouldn't appreciate his attempt at humor.

"Does this look to you like something I would sleep in?"

Remembering the demure cotton nightgown he'd seen her in, he couldn't hide his smile. "Um, no. Not really."

Lindsey riffled through everything in the suitcase before she stepped back and threw up her hands.

"I don't believe this."

Hoping to lighten the atmosphere a little, he walked over to his bag. "I can hardly wait to see what Mom and Ashley decided was the proper attire for a new husband visiting the tropics."

He lost all sign of his sense of humor once he opened the bag. There wasn't a pair of jeans, boots or a western shirt in the bunch. The trousers were khaki or cotton. There were a couple of dress shirts, trousers, a sports jacket and a few beachwear shorts, sneakers and flip-flops.

He looked grimly at Lindsey and saw that she was watching him. When she caught his eye, she nodded and said, "Well, at least we know what happened." He saw her mouth twitch.

"What?"

"We have the wrong luggage. I wonder who has ours?" And then she burst into laughter, sinking onto the bed and holding her sides.

He thought of the absurdity of the entire day that had culminated with strip-show attire for Lindsey and nerdy stuff for him, and joined her laughter.

Only her laughter didn't stop. It turned into sobs and he realized that she'd kept her nerves under control all day, despite his comments and disgruntlement, until everything became too much for her.

He felt lower than a snake. Regardless of the circumstances, nothing of this had been her fault. As she'd pointed out at the time, she hadn't been found in *his* bed. So why had he taken his frustration out on her?

She was doubled over, her forehead resting on her knees in an attempt to muffle the sound. Jared felt like a complete louse. He moved over to her and sat down beside her. She jerked away without looking at him.

"I'm sorry," he said quietly. He handed her his handkerchief, which she reluctantly accepted, and he waited. Eventually she straightened and turned her head away from him, furiously wiping at her face.

"What are *you* sorry for?" She sounded angry, which he could handle a lot more easily than her tears.

"For being a complete jerk."

She blew her nose. "If you're waiting for me to contradict you, you'll be waiting a long time." She went into the bathroom and shut the door.

Lindsey came out when the food arrived and they ate without speaking.

After they ate and she appeared to be calmer, Jared said, "I'm really not some prehistoric ape who will wait until you fall asleep to grab you." He held up his hand. "I solemnly promise."

The corners of her mouth lifted slightly.

"If you're not comfortable sleeping in one of those see-through nightgowns, I bet we can find something in my suitcase for you to wear. It may be gaudy as hell, but it would cover you."

He'd never seen her look more vulnerable than when she smiled at him and said, "Well, we seem to be continuing with all the traditions. Now I'm the bride who cried on her wedding night."

Jared chuckled. "That's usually what a bride does *after* sex, not instead of sex."

She punched his arm. "Are you *ever* serious?"

"I can be, but in this particular case we need to hang on to our senses of humor and not treat this like some kind of tragedy. We're here. We're married. We have two beds. We'll get some sleep, get up at an ungodly hour in order to get to the airport by four-thirty. We'll fly to Cancun, enjoy the sea, sand and surf, eat way too much, get great tans and come back home."

"Without sex." There was a hint of a question in her voice.

How was he to respond to that one? Hmm. "I tell you what," he finally said, "I'm going to leave that up to you. If you say yes I can promise you that it won't be about sex. I'll be making love to you. I assure you that I don't intend to claim any husbandly rights that you don't offer. But don't ever think that I don't want you, Lindsey."

She shifted and placed her arms around his neck. "Thank you," she said softly, and kissed him.

He placed his hands at her waist to remind himself not to touch her anywhere else while he followed her lead. When he responded, she seemed to gain some confidence, so that by the time she sat back from him, he was in bad shape with no hope of relief.

He moved away and stood. "I'll find you something to sleep in," he mumbled and went back to his bag. When he finally turned to face her, he had himself somewhat under control. He held out a T-shirt and a shirt that buttoned. "Take your pick," he said.

She took both of them and disappeared into the bathroom. A minute or so later he heard the shower running.

Great going, Crenshaw. Now you'll spend the week wondering if she's going to decide to make love with you or not. Be sure to enjoy your restful, relaxing week at the beach.

Eight

When the alarm went off a few hours later, Lindsey was surprised to discover that she'd been sound asleep. She would have sworn she'd be awake all night.

She reached for the alarm just as Jared hit the off button, and there was blessed silence. She waited for him to turn on the light.

When he didn't, she said tentatively, "Jared."

"Mmm," was his only reply.

"Do you mind if I turn on the light?"

"Wha—? Oh, sure." She heard him yawn.

Lindsey had slept in the T-shirt Jared had given her, which came to her knees. She'd appreciated his offer.

She turned on the light and sat on the side of the bed. Jared had his arm over his eyes and she smiled. Either he was giving her some privacy or protecting his eyes from the glare.

She gathered up the clothes she'd laid out to wear and hurried into the bathroom. As soon as she was dressed, she came out and said, "It's all yours."

She caught him in the middle of a stretch, his jeans low on his hips. How was it he could look so sexy in the morning, needing a shave and with his hair standing out in every direction?

"Thanks," he said and turned toward her. He did a double take. "Wow," he said quietly.

"What?"

"You look great in red. I like the dress, but aren't your shoulders going to be cold?"

Spaghetti straps were holding the dress on. "I'll wear my jacket until we get to Cancun."

He nodded, still looking at her. The dress was form-fitting to the waist, then swirled out into a very full skirt that stopped at her knees.

She crossed her arms over her chest. "This was the least revealing outfit they packed for me," she said abruptly.

"Oh! Sorry. Didn't mean to make you uncomfortable. It's just that—well, you just look so—" he threw up his hands "—sexy in that outfit. You're going to get mobbed as soon as men see you."

She walked over and picked up her jacket. "Somehow I doubt that very much." She slipped her arms into the light coat. "Better?"

He started to speak, stopped and strode toward the bathroom. He paused in the doorway and looked back at her. "Believe it or not, I meant everything that I said as a compliment, not to antagonize you. I'd really like to be able to get through a day around you without your getting all bent out of shape." As he closed the door behind him, he added, "Just a thought."

She stared at the closed door, squeezed her eyes shut and did her best to muffle her groan.

What was the matter with her, anyway? She wasn't normally so sensitive to compliments. The problem was that she was way out of her comfort zone. She'd always thought that when she decided to marry, the man she chose would be someone she'd known for ages, with whom she would be comfortable, and that the two of them would be friends as well as lovers.

She'd given no thought to spending any time with Jared Crenshaw. He made her nervous. She didn't like the way he made her feel when she was around him. All jittery and nervous. Off balance. All right, and naive, as well.

Now she wondered what she'd gotten herself into. She'd panicked when her dad had become so ill and she had wanted to make him happy. In other words, she'd fallen right back into her old pattern.

Only this time, someone else was inextricably involved as well.

After she closed her bag, she sat on the end of her bed and waited for Jared to appear. He'd put on his jeans, shirt and boots. As soon as he walked out, the scent of aftershave wafting around him, she said, "I'm sorry. You're absolutely right. I'm being ridiculous, overreacting to everything you say." She stood and held out her hand. "Pax?"

He looked at her hand. "All right," he said slowly, giving it a quick shake and immediately releasing it. "And I've got to admit I'm not at my best at—" he looked at his watch "—four-thirty in the morning, so I figure we're even." In a brisk tone he said, "The airport is a couple of minutes away. We can leave the car here and they'll keep an eye on it and shuttle us to the airport. Do you have everything?"

She nodded. He picked up their bags and motioned with his head for her to lead the way.

Once the plane leveled off in the air, Jared leaned his seat back and closed his eyes. Lindsey sat by the window and watched the clouds and the glimpses of water as they cleared the Texas coast.

She returned to the thoughts that had kept her awake for most of the night—making love with Jared.

She couldn't argue with the fact that this week would be agonizingly awkward, if last night was any example. Even with two beds, they would be sharing a room and a bath.

Lindsey admitted to herself how attracted she was to the man. She'd found him fascinating while they were dating, and his kisses had let her know that she was vulnerable where he was concerned. Now they were married. Why shouldn't she explore the feelings he aroused in her? They had a week of privacy and he'd made *his* feelings on the subject plain enough. There was no reason for her to get so uptight about their situation.

She'd never been tempted to make love to any of the men she'd dated in college and since her graduation, and no one had ever gotten out of line. Perhaps that was because she was R. W. Russell's daughter.

Jared was the only man she'd met who didn't appear to be intimidated by her father or his position. His offer of marriage hadn't been because of her dad's attitude, but because he'd wanted to do the right thing by her.

They both deserved this time away from their real lives. A fantasy week with a handsome, virile man began to have more and more appeal for her.

* * *

Jared stirred about an hour before landing. He glanced over at Lindsey and she smiled. Oh, yes. Definitely a man she wanted to know better, in bed and out. With her decision made, Lindsey allowed herself to appreciate his good looks, his great body and his unforgettable smile.

"What are you looking at?" he asked, a slight crease appearing between his brows.

"Oh, I've been going through the packet Dad gave us. There's quite a brochure about the hotel. I'm impressed."

"What does it say?"

In the chirpy voice of an eager travel agent, Lindsey read, "A perfect getaway for adults only. Private beaches, several restaurants, honeymoon suites."

His frown increased. "Honeymoon suites?" He closed his eyes. "Great."

She continued reading in her own voice. "Honeymooners receive a complimentary candlelight dinner their first evening. Champagne, a flower arrangement and a fruit basket are part of the hotel's welcome."

He opened his eyes. "Champagne, huh?"

"Mmm. I don't drink very often, but this sounds like a nice offer."

Jared stretched. "I'll be right back," he said, and walked to the back of the plane.

Once inside the tiny restroom he stared at himself in the mirror. *Why don't they shoot me now and put me out of my misery?* Candlelight dinner, champagne, honeymoon suite. Everything a man could want or need to set up a great seduction scene.

What a waste.

He pictured Lindsey wearing one of those see-through gowns, holding a flute of champagne, and his mouth grew dry.

"Stiff upper lip, old chap," he told himself. Unfortunately, that wasn't the only thing that would remain stiff for the rest of their stay.

Once they landed and cleared customs, Jared carried their bags to a taxi stand where they got a ride to the resort.

When they turned into the private drive of the hotel where they would be staying, Lindsey gasped in awe. "Just look, Jared. This place looks like a tropical paradise."

"Yeah, I noticed." He felt like ramming his fists into a punching bag a few dozen times. In an effort to appear civil, he added, "Really nice."

He was surprised when she reached for his hand and said, "This is going to be so much fun, Jared. Let's enjoy every minute of it!"

Her enthusiasm left him speechless. Maybe she didn't enjoy sex. Maybe she—naw, don't go there. She'd been quite responsive whenever he'd kissed her. Who knew what her problem was? He was too busy dealing with his.

Once they checked in, they received several brochures describing activities they might enjoy.

Jared glanced through them while they rode the elevator to the top floor. When the door opened, the porter led them down a long hallway to the last door. With a flourish, the porter opened the door and carried the luggage inside. Jared pulled out a couple of bills and handed them to him, nodding when the man thanked him.

He wasn't surprised, when he looked around the room, to discover the suite looked like something from a Hollywood movie.

There was only one, rather massive, bed. After all, it was a room for honeymooners. There was a sitting area and a fully equipped bathroom nearby. He opened doors and discovered a nice-size closet and yet another bathroom. At least they could have some privacy some of the time. This one had a huge tub with water jets. He could think of all kinds of things to do.

Don't go there.

When he finished his exploring, he walked over to Lindsey who stood at one of the windows, looking out. He stopped beside her and put his hands into his back pockets.

"Nice view," he said, determined to be polite even if it killed him.

She glanced around at him, a huge grin on her face. "Nice? More like absolutely gorgeous."

"True," he agreed, although his gaze was on her. Her dress blew him away. Shorter than her usual style and much more colorful, the dress swirled around her knees when she walked and drew the eye to her shapely legs and ankles.

She'd chosen to leave her hair down this morning and the combination of the dress and casual hairdo, along with her sexy good looks, kept him aroused.

"So what would you like to do now?" he finally asked.

She thought for a moment. "Let's change clothes and go to the beach. I can hardly wait to play in the water. What do you say?"

He shrugged. "Fine."

"This is going to be fun, Jared. Let's enjoy our time here, okay?"

"Not a problem." If he kept saying that often enough, maybe he'd be able to convince himself.

Nine

Lindsey went into one of the bathrooms to change while Jared went into the other one.

After holding up the three swimsuits, she made a note to herself to go shopping immediately. She finally settled on the one-piece. It had a halter top with a V-neck that plunged between her breasts. The back was practically non-existent, barely covering her bottom.

She quickly pulled on a pair of shorts and a scoop-neck T-shirt.

She gathered lotion and towels into a beach bag and returned to the bedroom.

Jared had changed into a pair of shorts that revealed his firm butt and muscular legs. He'd pulled a shirt on but left it open. With some grumbling, he put on a pair of sandals, muttering something about hoping he didn't run into anyone he knew in this getup.

The first thing Lindsey noticed when they walked out onto the beach was the number of women who were alone. Each of them appeared to be eyeing Jared as though he were alone, as well.

Lindsey found their gazes to be irritating. Not that it really mattered. She had no reason to feel in the least possessive. Whatever happened here in Cancun wouldn't change anything. As long as she went into an affair—with her own husband, yet!—with her eyes wide open, she wouldn't get hurt.

Jared spread out a large beach towel, provided by the resort, beneath one of the umbrellas. "Ready?" he asked, and she nodded. He stripped down to his suit and she did the same.

They eyed each other speculatively.

As though in silent agreement not to comment on one another's appearance, they walked toward the water. The water felt like satin against Lindsey's skin.

"Do you plan to swim?" Jared asked.

"No, I'm going to stay here and paddle around some, then stretch out in the sun."

She watched the muscles of his back and shoulders flex as he continued into deeper water. He did a surface dive and disappeared from her view.

Lindsey was now faced with how to tell Jared that she wanted to make love with him. It wasn't something she could casually blurt out. Maybe she could figure out a way to show him.

Eventually she returned to their umbrella and sat down. After she'd dried off, Lindsey rubbed suntan lotion on most of her exposed areas, put on her sunglasses and looked for Jared.

His blond hair made him easy to spot. When he finally left the water and walked toward her, he was breathing hard. Quite a workout. He probably needed it after sitting for a large part of the day.

She handed him a towel after he dropped down next to her. Once he was dry, she said, "Let me put some suntan lotion on your back and shoulders so you don't burn. The reflection off the water is just as potent as direct sunlight."

He gave her a long, steady look and she returned it with an innocent smile. "Okay," he finally said. He stretched out on his stomach and rested his head on his folded arms.

She dribbled lotion along the indentation of his spine. He tensed.

"Is it cold?"

"No."

She smoothed her hands over his back, from the nape of his neck to the waistband of his swimsuit. Next, she poured lotion into her palm, rubbed her hands together and began to knead his neck and shoulders, eliciting a pleasured groan from him. She continued to work on the muscles of his back and was dismayed to realize that the mere act of touching him aroused her. How embarrassing. All-girl schools until college, together with her father's watchful eye, had given her little experience in an intimate setting with a man. Now she could touch him with impunity, explore the curves and contours of his broad back. She was fascinated by the way his wide shoulders tapered into a narrow waist.

Now she could sleep with him for a week—with all that implied—without guilt. If she had the nerve.

Her problem was how to let him know that she wanted to make love with him.

When she'd finished Jared's massage, he was sound

asleep and her body quivered with need. On impulse, she decided to get in the water and swim a little, hoping to get control of herself.

When she left, he didn't stir.

The sun neared the western horizon when Jared opened his eyes. He immediately sat up and looked around. Foot traffic on the beach had lightened considerably since he fell asleep.

He glanced at Lindsey, who was curled on her side, asleep. He reached to wake her when he recalled his new rule—no touching.

"Lindsey?"

"Mmm?"

"It's getting late. We need to go back to the hotel."

As soon as she opened her eyes she sat up. "I didn't mean to go to sleep."

"Neither did I, but it doesn't matter. We're here to rest and relax and, so far, our first day here has been a success."

They put on the clothes they'd worn, gathered up towels and her beach bag and walked to the path that led to the hotel.

On the way to the elevators Lindsey paused in front of a large display of colorful brochures. "Look, Jared, Dad's packet didn't have all of this."

He picked up one of them and studied it. "You want to go swim with the dolphins?" he asked, handing her the brochure.

"Might be fun."

"There's a boat excursion going to Islas Mujeres where they offer all kinds of things, including seeing the dolphins." He flipped through a couple more. "We can also rent a car for the day and explore some of the Mayan ruins, if you'd like."

"I really don't care what we do," she said. She stared

out at the large swimming pool where several couples were lounging, a waiter moving among them with exotic drinks. Finally, she turned back and looked at Jared. "I just realized something—I've never taken a real vacation before. My travels have been carefully planned and supervised. I love the idea of having so much free time to spend doing whatever we choose."

Maybe this marriage was exactly what Lindsey needed to escape her father's heavy-handed protection. From something the senator had said at the wedding reception, Jared got the impression that he expected Lindsey to continue to live with him while Jared was overseas.

Boy, was he in for a surprise.

Once in their room, Jared ordered dinner. Then each of them gathered up fresh clothing and went into the bathrooms.

While Jared showered, he reviewed the rules he'd come up with while he'd exhausted himself swimming.

Rule number one—no touching and, especially, no kissing.

Number two—no sleeping in the same bed with Lindsey. The sofa was too short for his long legs. Maybe he'd rig up a couple of the chairs, or as a last resort, the floor would work.

He reminded himself that he'd been in much tougher positions than this in his life. Dangerous ones. Even life-threatening, physically daunting situations. He'd handled them because he was a survivor.

He could certainly survive a week without touching his new bride.

Once dressed, he felt better about their situation. The massage and nap had been just what he'd needed to get into a better frame of mind.

He'd survive whatever came his way by being adaptable. They'd plan a week full of sightseeing and swimming that would tire them. They'd spend minimum time in the room. He could do this.

When Jared walked out of the bathroom, he knew he could handle his situation. That is, until he saw Lindsey.

Lindsey was nervous. She wanted to be subtle with her message that she wanted to make love to him. She wasn't certain that her choice of apparel was particularly subtle.

What if he laughed? Or worse, ignored her hint. She couldn't see herself telling him outright.

She stood looking out at the lights on the beach and the way the surf glowed white in the darkness. When she heard the door open, she turned and looked at him.

He'd stopped abruptly when he saw her, his face growing grim.

She swallowed. "I believe our dinner should be here any minute now. I hope you're hungry."

He cleared his throat. "You have no idea," he said gruffly. He stuck his hands into the pockets of his khaki pants and walked to another window, seemingly fascinated by the view.

When a knock sounded on the door, he said, "You might not want the waiter ogling you, which I can assure you, he will."

Her face grew hot. Without a word she returned to the bathroom and closed the door, weakly leaning against it and staring into the mirrored wall in front of her.

Well, he'd definitely noticed that she'd worn one of the nightgown-and-robe sets she'd brought with her, a decision she'd made while they were at the beach. And he was right—she wouldn't want anyone but Jared to see her in this. He'd studiously looked away from her after the first shock of seeing her dressed so provocatively.

Did he understand what she was attempting to convey? If he did, he hadn't let on.

She sighed. *Let's face it. You're just not the* femme fatale *type.*

Jared tapped on the door. "You can come out now," he said.

Lindsey felt a moment of panic. Should she change into something else? Ignore the fact that her wardrobe hid very little from the imagination?

She lifted her chin. No. She'd carry this out, no matter what.

Lindsey opened the door and walked into the room.

Flickering flames from candles were reflected in the windows that sunset had turned into mirrors.

A table by the windows had been set with plates and votives. Indirect lighting was the only other illumination in the room. A bottle of champagne, nestled in a tub of ice, sat on a small stand nearby. Music played from hidden speakers and the savory scent of dinner wafted across the room to her.

The scene was set for seduction. Well, she was doing her best.

Jared pulled out a chair for her. Once she sat down, he moved her closer to the table. "Everything looks delicious. This is so romantic."

"Oh, yeah, I'll definitely agree with that." He opened the champagne and filled two of the glasses. He held his out, "Happy honeymoon, Lindsey."

She wished he looked happier saying that than he did. She touched the rim of her glass to his. "Thank you." She sipped and smiled. The champagne tasted delicious.

Lindsey continued to sip on her champagne while they

ate, mostly in silence. Jared kept her glass filled and she was grateful. It helped to settle her nerves and give her more of a sense of freedom.

While they ate dessert and had coffee, she said, "You're probably wondering why I chose to wear this tonight."

He glanced up and his eyes mirrored the flames of the candles. "You look very—uh—very nice. That color looks good on you."

"It's peach."

"Uh-huh." He reached for his glass of champagne and finished it in one swallow.

"I feel so awkward. I've never owned anything remotely like this, but it's appropriate for the occasion, don't you think?"

He stared at her as though she'd lost her mind.

"What I'm trying to say is that, well, we're married and, uh, we're going to be here a week, so I don't—" she stopped and coughed "—see why we shouldn't treat it as a real honeymoon."

There. She'd said it.

His eyes narrowed. "Are you saying what I think you're saying?"

She nodded.

"You want us to make love," he said slowly.

She nodded.

He slowly leaned back in his chair, a smile forming on his lips. "No kidding?"

"I don't kid about a thing like that."

His smile turned into a grin. "So your gown is to get me in the mood."

She nodded.

"Just so you know, you could have worn a nun's habit and I would still be in the mood." In a moment, he added, "Wow."

She watched him nervously. "Then you're agreeable to the idea? It won't change our agreement?"

"Yes. No."

They laughed and he reached for her hand. "I think you're absolutely right. We'll do all the things that honeymooners do, enjoy the sights, go home and continue with our agreement."

"So," she said slowly, "what do we do next?"

He gave her a wicked grin. "Well, it seems to me that we've had a really long day and that we should probably go to bed soon. Like now."

"Now?" she repeated faintly. "Oh. Okay."

They stood. "Just so you know," he added, "if you decide to change your mind about this, I'll stop at any time. I don't want any misunderstandings here."

She took a deep breath. "Thank you."

He walked around the table and slipped his arms around her. "Since this is my first honeymoon, I don't know what we do next, either. So I think we should wing it. What would you like to do next?"

"A kiss would be nice," she said, sounding breathless. The next thing she knew, he was kissing her as if all of his restraints had been removed. That's when she knew everything would be okay.

Jared picked her up and carried her to the enormous bed. Talk about being adaptable—he was more than ready to forget his carefully made rules.

Did she have any idea how delectable she looked in that outfit? He'd had trouble keeping his eyes off her during dinner and had already been planning another shower when they finished. A long one. A very cold one.

He placed her on the bed and straightened up, breaking

the record for shedding his clothes, then stretched out beside her.

"Do you want me to take this off now?"

Ah. The tremor in her voice gave her away. "Lindsey?"

"Yes."

"I need to ask you something."

She looked alarmed. "Okay."

"Is this going to be your first time?"

She frowned. "Is that going to be a problem?"

He couldn't help smiling. She was always so serious. "Not at all. It just tells me what I need to know to make it as pleasant as possible."

"I'm not ignorant of the process, you know," she replied, sounding a little miffed.

All he had to do was laugh and he'd be sleeping on the floor from now on. Very seriously, he said, "Of course you aren't. I just don't want to hurt you, that's all."

"Oh."

He placed his hand on her abdomen and it was the only thing that kept her from hitting the ceiling. "It's okay," he said soothingly. "We've got all night. All week, for that matter. I just want you to relax."

"I am," she said, her eyes watching him closely.

"Good. I'd like to touch you and to get to know you, to—"

"We've already been introduced, Jared. Let's just do it, okay?"

He was quiet for a moment. Finally, he said, "Why don't we get into the tub and turn the jet sprays on."

"Now?" She sounded horrified.

"It'll be fun, I promise." He got up and said, "I'll go start the water and be right back." When he returned he pulled her to him and then rolled onto his back so that she was on top of him. "Can you feel how very much I want you?"

She nodded.

"I've been in this condition since the first time we met. What I'm trying to say is, I want you too much and I don't want to hurt you. I think the hot tub will be relaxing for both of us."

She moved her hips experimentally and smiled when he hissed. "If you insist," she said reluctantly, and slowly slid off him. Ah, so she was beginning to get a taste of her own power in this situation.

Good. He went into the bathroom and turned off the water. "Care to join me?" he called. He turned on the jets and let the water cool *his* jets a little.

Lindsey appeared in the doorway after having removed what little she'd had covering her. She was exquisite. Nothing showy and yet, he'd never seen a sexier woman. He wanted her so badly, he ached. Literally.

She came in and hurriedly slid into the tub, sitting opposite him.

"Isn't this nice?"

She shrugged. "It's okay. It's not exactly what I was expecting, but it's okay."

"See, this is where all the reading and listening to lectures doesn't really explain about making love. It can be done anywhere—not just in bed."

"Like in the back seat of a car."

"Exactly."

"My roommate in high school got pregnant that way."

"Believe me, the car wasn't to blame."

She chuckled and he could see her beginning to relax a little. "So this is your idea of foreplay, I take it?"

"One of them."

"You have more?"

He grinned. Damn, but she was fun to tease. "Stick with me kid, and you'll deserve a degree in higher learning after all the things I'll show you this week."

"I see your ego made the trip all right."

He laughed, feeling better than he had in a long, long while. He hadn't turned the overhead light on, thinking it would help her to relax. Instead, he'd lit a couple of pillar candles on the counter. They were reflected in all the mirrors in the room.

The frothing water hid her high, round breasts from his view, but that was all right. He intended to do a great deal more than look, anyway.

The warm, relaxing water eventually worked its magic and he watched her sink bonelessly down until she was chin deep.

"We seem to have a small problem here, though."

Her weighted eyelids slowly opened. "What's wrong?"

"You're much too far away."

She blushed, just as he knew she would. He straightened enough to reach her hand, then he gave a little tug that caused her to glide through the water toward him. He turned her so that she had her back pressed against his chest. "Ah, that's better."

The mirrors reflected the contrasts between them—his blond hair, her dark hair. His height, her smallness. The gleam in his eyes, the wariness appearing in hers.

"Just relax," he whispered near her ear.

She caught his eye in the mirror and made a face at him. "How do I do that when a part of your anatomy is pushing against me?"

"He's just being playful, that's all."

"Of course he is."

He lifted his hands off the side of the tub and cupped her breasts. "Mmm, very nice."

She gave a start and then he could feel her forcing herself to relax.

He stroked and massaged her, gently capturing her nipples between his fingers and tugging on them until they hardened into little pebbles. Her breathing changed into quick little gasps, which reassured him that she was being affected by what he was doing.

Eventually, he began to massage her shoulders. "You deserve a massage after the wonderful one I received." Then he placed his hands on either side of her and followed the contours of her waist and hips. He stopped moving them—momentarily—once he reached her knees.

Lindsey squirmed against him, pushing against his hard arousal.

With a lazy motion he moved his hands to the insides of her knees and slowly stroked them, moving up to her inner thighs. She squeezed her knees together, trapping his hands at the tops of her thighs.

He brushed his thumb back and forth across the hidden nub of flesh between her legs. She moaned and relaxed her legs, allowing him further access.

Jared teased her, slipping a finger into her, then moving it away, until she pushed against his hand, silently signaling for more.

He obliged her.

When she finally turned to face him, he was more than ready for her. He slid forward to give her legs room and pulled them over his thighs. She reached for his solid length, her hands trembling as she explored. He reached for her and lifted her until he was directly below her. She reached for his shoulders as he ever so slowly lowered her onto him, his arms quivering with the effort.

As soon as she felt him, her eyes flew open. "Oh!"

He stopped. "Does that hurt?"

Her glazed eyes stared sightlessly at him. "It feels so different from what I expected. It's huge."

"Thank you for the compliment, ma'am, but the truth is you are very small."

She dropped her head on his shoulder and rocked against him. How could he possibly ignore that?

He carefully entered her, moving slightly, then pulled away slightly. She frowned. He continued to move in and out until he was finally and fully sheathed deep inside her. He could no longer muffle the groan of pleasure he felt now that he was, at long last, inside of her.

She pressed against him, her arms wrapped around his neck.

"Am I hurting you?" he asked.

She shook her head.

"Do you want to get back in bed now?"

She raised her head, her face inches from his. "If you dare stop what you're doing, I won't be responsible for my actions," she said, panting. "But take my word for it, it won't be pretty."

He laughed and kissed her. He lifted her hips slightly and moved her as he thrust into her, his movements as slow as he could possibly make them. He could feel beads of sweat collecting on his brow and running down the side of his face, no doubt due to the temperature of the water and having nothing to do with the intense rein he held against his body's need for completion.

The kiss continued, his tongue in rhythm with his other movement until Lindsey let out a cry and started moving rapidly against him. He could hold back no longer. He held her tightly, moving her quickly against him until she froze, her body convulsing around him. He groaned and went over the edge with her.

When Jared finally became aware of their surroundings once again, the only sound besides their harsh breathing was the water gently bubbling around them. He waited until he felt that his legs would hold them both, and stood. He stepped out of the tub, still holding Lindsey, flipped off the switch for the jets, opened the drain and blew out the candles.

He loved the feel of her body draped loosely against him. He picked up the towel she'd used earlier and quickly wiped most of the water off them before he returned to the bedroom.

Moonlight shone through the windows, lighting a path to the bed. He lowered her onto the bed and came down on top of her.

"Wow," she said.

He kept his weight on his forearms. "At the very least." He placed small kisses over her face, around her ears and along her graceful neck.

"I had no idea," she finally said.

"Frankly," he said, a little unnerved by the realization, "neither did I."

His mouth sought hers and there was no more conversation. He was teaching her other communication skills. He was delighted with her interest in learning.

Late morning sun crept over them until the light hit Jared's face. He turned his head away, slowly coming awake enough to realize it was daylight. They'd made love most of the night, although he'd chosen other ways to love her that wouldn't make her any more sore.

He'd shown her there were many ways for a man and a woman to pleasure each other, all equally satisfying.

He lay on his side, with Lindsey curled up spoon fashion next to him. His hand cupped her breast and he smiled. Even in his sleep he hadn't let go of her.

He trailed his fingers down her side, past her ribs, down to her waist and up the flare of her hips. She didn't stir.

He felt quite primitively possessive this morning, and grinned. He'd better keep that particular thought to himself. Lindsey prized her independence now that she'd finally made a giant step away from her father.

The marriage had worked out for both of them. She got what she wanted and he'd placated the senator for his family's sake.

This morning, he didn't feel much like a sacrificial lamb. This whole thing was going to work out well for both of them.

Jared eased out of bed and went to have a shower and shave. He'd be shaving twice a day this week to make certain he didn't hurt her delicate skin.

After a leisurely breakfast, they put on their swimsuits and went down to the beach. This time, Lindsey wore one of the bikinis and its matching beach cover. They weren't the only ones with the same idea. Jared spread out a large beach towel provided by the resort beneath one of the umbrellas.

Lindsey stood watching the muscles of his back and shoulders flex as he knelt. She'd learned his body last night with her lips and fingertips but he was even more gorgeous in the sun, stripped down to his swimsuit.

She knelt beside him and removed her beach cover. "You might as well not be wearing any clothes," he said, frowning at her suit. She liked that possessive look in his eyes but she would never admit it—he'd be even more arrogant and smug, if that were possible.

She had a hunch that she was being taught by a master of bedroom arts. She'd known from the night they'd met that he could affect her like no other man ever had. Now that she'd made love with him, she couldn't help but wonder if she'd be able to make love with another man once they'd split up.

Of course she would. Don't get all mushy at this point in your life. You're on your way to New York, with only a small detour that was proving to be quite wonderful. Ego or not, Jared had shown her a few things that none of the books she'd read had ever touched on.

She smiled at the memory.

Jared reached for the sunblock. "You're going to burn quickly with so much skin that's never been exposed to the sun before." He poured lotion into his palms, rubbed them together and rubbed his hands across her chest, his fingers slipping beneath the flimsy fabric that barely covered her breasts.

"Jared!" She reached for his wrist. "We're in public!"

"So?" he asked innocently. "I'm just putting lotion on. There's nothing wrong with that."

She laughed. "Well, I think I can handle the front without your help." She turned her back to him. "How about you work back there?"

"You're no fun at all."

She peeked over her shoulder, grinning. "Really? Now that surprises me. You didn't say anything like that last night."

"Has anyone mentioned that you have a smart mouth?"

"No."

"That's because you hide it so well beneath that regal air of yours."

"What are you talking about?"

"Lie down, so I can do your legs, as well." He stroked down her legs, from the high rise on the sides of her bikini bottom to her ankles. "You have this air about you that reminds me of a member of some royal family. You look quite aloof and self-contained. However, last night you proved that underneath that facade is a tiger-lady. I couldn't be happier with the discovery."

He massaged her calves and worked his way up her thighs, gently rubbing as he slid his hands along her upper inner thigh, one of his fingers straying until he slipped it inside her. She jerked and glared at him over her shoulder. "I don't need lotion there!"

He stood and pulled her up with him. "You might. Let's go try out the water." When they reached the shallows he picked her up and raced into the water, with her clinging to his neck and squealing. He didn't stop until he was chest high.

She clung to his neck and looked around. "This is over my head, you know."

He grinned, a wicked gleam in his eyes. "Don't worry, I won't let you drown. Here, let's get you a little more comfortable, shall we?" He turned her toward him and eased her legs around his hips.

"You can't be," she said, blushing.

"Ready to make love to you? Guess again."

"But...but there's all these people around and..."

"And no one can see a thing except that you have your arms around my shoulders." He pushed aside the thin scrap of material between her legs and eased into her.

She closed her eyes and groaned. She seemed to stay embarrassingly wet inside whenever he was around.

He cupped her bottom, holding her close to him. "Comfy?" he asked, his eyes dancing.

"You're insatiable," she replied and kissed him.

By the time the kiss ended, he was moving rapidly within her and she clung to him, feeling her body grow tighter and tighter until she gave a keening cry. He buried himself deeply inside of her and shook.

Lindsey relaxed against him, loving the feel of him inside her. She closed her eyes and smiled. Nothing so healthy as a little sun, sea and sex to make a honeymoon complete.

"Oh, Jared, I've never experienced anything so exciting, so compelling, so…I can't find the words to express myself. All I know is that this morning has been the most memorable time of my life. I will never forget it."

They were having lunch together at an outdoor café after a fun-filled morning on Islas Mujeres.

"I can certainly see where you've placed me in the scheme of things. I'm not as memorable as swimming with the dolphins, huh?" He was on a high, too, but his was caused by the joy of seeing her bubbling over with enthusiasm. She'd metamorphosed into an enthusiastic woman eager to explore all the sights, unafraid to show her emotions. She laughed easily and had more than once initiated a session of heavy-duty lovemaking this week.

The senator wouldn't recognize the woman seated across from him.

She wrinkled her nose at him. "You know what I mean. How many people are given a chance to be so close to those marvelous creatures? The way they look at you with such intelligence and knowing, as though they already understand all the secrets of the universe."

"I'm glad you enjoyed it," he replied, smiling at her. With her deepening tan, she was beginning to look like some of the natives. Almost Polynesian.

"I will always have a special place in my heart for them," she said a few minutes later with a pleased sigh.

They continued their meal.

"The week's almost over," she said when they finished. "I'm amazed at how quickly the days have passed."

"I hadn't realized how much I needed to get away from the real world until we got down here."

"The real world. Yes, it's definitely at the other end of our flight home."

"You've only got a few weeks now until you'll be heading North. Don't forget your parka and snowshoes."

"The weather will be considerably different from here, that's a fact."

"So, are you ready to go back to the mainland?"

She nodded. "I think so. If we're going to the Mayan ruins tomorrow, we're going to have a full day."

"We don't have to go, you know."

"Yes, we do. Tomorrow's our last full day here and I don't want to leave here without seeing some of them."

They left the café and wandered toward the shore where they'd find a way across the water.

"You're really tired, huh?" he asked, once they were on their way.

She turned her head slowly and gave him a provocative look. "What did you have in mind, sailor?"

He grabbed her and, despite the interested onlookers, gave her a rather passionate kiss that resolved the issue of how they would spend their afternoon.

Ten

Jared and Lindsey arrived back at Jared's home late Sunday evening. They were both tired from traveling and the normal letdown of having to return to their real lives. Lindsey had fallen asleep before they left Austin and didn't stir when he turned off the engine.

He smiled and reached over, rubbing her cheek with the back of his knuckles.

"Hey, sleepyhead, we're home."

Lindsey's lashes fluttered and she slowly opened her eyes. As soon as she focused on him, she smiled. "Home? Already?" she asked.

He chuckled. "Since you were asleep by the time we left the airport, I guess it did seem like a short drive."

She sat up, stretched and looked around, yawning. "What time is it?"

"A little after midnight."

"I'll probably be awake for the rest of the night."

"Can I count on that?" he asked, nibbling her ear. She turned her head, searching for his mouth. When they broke apart, Jared said, "We can unload the car tomorrow. Let's go to bed."

When he opened his front door, Jared almost tripped over the boxes stacked nearby. He flipped on the switch and looked around.

"Oh! Someone brought my things here while we've been gone. How nice."

Jared frowned. "I wonder why they didn't stack them in a corner, out of the way."

She turned and slipped her arms around him. "We can move them first thing in the morning."

He swung her into his arms, and she wrapped her legs around his waist. "Maybe not *first* thing," he said, striding across the living room and down the hall to his bedroom.

He made short work of getting them undressed. Once in bed, he leaned over her, trailing kisses along her jaw and neck until he reached her breasts. "I've been having withdrawal symptoms all day."

She sounded breathless when she replied. "Why?"

"Because this is the longest I've gone without making love to you since our first night in Cancun."

She drew in a sharp breath when his lips surrounded one of her nipples and tugged on it. "The honeymoon is over. We can't spend as much time in bed as we did all week."

He raised his head. "Sure we can."

Lindsey must have agreed with him because there was no more talking—just whispers, sighs and groans of pleasure.

The next morning while Lindsey made breakfast, Jared moved her belongings to the bedroom they had intended for her to use.

After his last trip into the bedroom, he paused and sightlessly stared out the window.

He was going to miss her. The better he got to know her, the more he liked her. Well, more than liked her. His feelings where she was concerned were confusing. Their week together hadn't been all fun and games. They'd spent time talking about their lives and what they wanted for the future. They'd spent hours when they were comfortably silent, just enjoying each other's company.

As often as they'd made love, he should be content. And he was. Wasn't he? They had an agreement—they'd go their separate ways after the holidays.

He reminded himself that he was the one who hadn't planned to marry anytime soon. Nothing had happened to change his mind.

They could remain friends, at least. He'd like that. He would want to know how she liked working at the museum. They could always e-mail each other. He wasn't sure why he didn't find that so appealing.

Snap out of it. Everything is going as planned.

They were seated on his back porch sometime around one o'clock—Jared didn't have on his watch, so he wasn't sure—when they heard a knock at the front door.

He looked at her. "Our first caller. At least they waited until a decent hour to come barging in. I'll see who it is."

She followed him into the living room and watched as he opened the front door.

Jared was a little surprised to see his dad, who smiled when he saw him. But only with his lips—his eyes had a grim look about them that caused a frisson of unease.

"Hi, Dad. Come on in."

"Your trip agreed with you," Joe said, stepping inside.

"You look rested and more tanned than usual." He saw Lindsey and nodded. "You look equally rested, Lindsey. Did you enjoy Cancun?"

"Very much. We took lots of photographs. There's way too much to see there in just a week."

"Sit down, Dad. Would you like some iced tea?"

"No, thanks. I can't stay long."

He sat in one of the chairs facing the sofa, so Jared motioned for Lindsey to join him on the couch. They sat a discreet foot apart. The shift in their relationship wasn't any of his dad's business, even if the man cared.

Joe leaned forward and placed his elbows on his knees. "I've got some news for you, Jared."

"Okay."

"I hired an investigator who found the man you met in the bar that night."

"Really! Why, that's great, Dad. What did he have to say for himself?"

"You had it pretty well worked out. He slipped something in your drink. Then he drove you to the Russell ranch and put you in bed with Lindsey."

"But that's crazy. Why would he do that?" she asked.

Joe studied her in silence for a moment, then softly said, "Good question, Lindsey. Maybe you could explain that to us."

She looked at him with a bewildered expression. Jared had a sinking sensation in his stomach. He had a hunch he didn't want to know what his dad had discovered.

"I'm sorry. I have no idea what you're talking about," Lindsey said.

"All right. I can accept that. Can you tell us why your father would hire a man to put Jared in bed with you?"

Jared couldn't help it. He stared at her as though he

didn't know her at all. Was it possible that she'd been a part of that? The thought turned his stomach.

"My father!" She came to her feet in a rush. "How can you say something like that? My father would never stoop to such a thing. If this man is trying to pin his actions on my father, then he's a liar."

She turned and walked out of the room. A moment later, the back door closed and he knew she'd returned to the back porch.

"Is there any doubt?" Jared had to ask.

"No. The man explained how, once the two of them got you undressed and into bed, the senator gave him a ride back to get his own car. The man never asked for a reason for doing it, and the senator didn't offer one. However, he paid him a healthy amount of money for his efforts."

"That son of a—" Jared could no longer sit. He stood and began to pace. "I can't believe that bastard had the gall to set me up like that. And then demand that I marry his daughter!"

"After I got the report, I discussed the whole matter with your mother, who was appalled to hear it and furious that I was only then telling her about it. So we're both in the doghouse about that one. She has a good head on her shoulders, Gail does. She thinks the senator must have wanted his daughter married off to a Crenshaw and you happened to be available."

"That's ridiculous."

"Think about it. As controlling and manipulative as the man has been in other matters, why wouldn't he decide to choose his daughter's husband without bothering to consult either party?"

Jared fought the rage that threatened to overcome him. The senator had been behind all of it. Had Lindsey been a part of the whole episode? Her righteous indignation just now, as well as at the scene in the café, could be sincere. Either that, or she was a great actress.

"I'm sorry to be the one who had to tell you. I've got the investigator's report in the truck, if you want it."

"Yeah, I'd like to see it."

They walked outside and Joe opened the door to his truck, reached inside and came out with a large manila envelope. He handed it to Jared. "I don't know how much this changes things for you. As I recall, you two plan to split when you come back from Saudi, don't you?"

Jared turned the envelope around in his hands. "That's the plan. I see no reason to change it."

Joe laid his hand on Jared's shoulder. "I want to apologize for jumping to conclusions that morning."

"Hell, who wouldn't have? It makes sense now that he wanted you to witness the setup and add your weight behind the pressure on us to get married."

"You've certainly got grounds for annulment. You could probably file a complaint of kidnapping against him."

"I know you're kidding, Dad. The sooner all of this is behind me, the better."

"I guess you at least got an expensive vacation out of all this. I just hope it was worth being hoodwinked."

"I don't like being made a fool of." Jared looked away. "It's a good thing I don't know where he is right now because I wouldn't be responsible for my actions." He looked back at Joe. "Have you told him that we know?"

"Nope. The information is yours to do with as you wish." He got into his truck and said, "Oh, and there's one more thing."

"What now?" Jared asked wearily.

"Your mother would like to have a word with you."

The two men looked at each other and, for the first time since he'd heard his father's news, Jared smiled. Thank goodness for family. "Tell her I'll see her soon, okay?"

He watched his dad drive away, looked at the envelope in his hand and walked over to his truck, which was parked nearby. He pulled a few papers out and scanned them. The man—Ted Harper—had been candid in his discussion. He told the P.I. step by step how the senator had approached him and asked him to help him with something. Harper was quoted as saying he thought he was just helping to play a practical joke and that he hoped he wasn't in any trouble.

He knew details that only the man who'd done it could know, and Jared could think of no reason for Harper to lie about the man who'd hired him. The P.I. had shown him a photo of Russell and Harper had confirmed that he was the man who'd hired him.

So now he knew.

Jared folded the papers and put them into his back pocket. As long as he was outside, he decided to unload the car. After putting the bags in the bedroom, he went around to the back porch. Lindsey sat there, staring into the distance.

He climbed the steps and sat down next to where he'd left his glass of tea. The ice had almost melted, but it didn't matter. He emptied the glass before he carefully set it on the table between them.

"You know," Lindsey said calmly without looking at him, "for some reason you and your family are determined to smear my father's reputation."

"I have the report right here, if you want to read it." He leaned forward, pulled it out of his pocket and placed it on the table.

"Oh, I'm sure that the man told your father's investigator exactly what he wanted to hear."

"The man was there, Lindsey. I remember that much. And he knows too many details not to be telling the truth."

"Except for who hired him, of course." She stood and walked to the back door. "I'm sure you're relieved that our farce of a marriage is effectively over."

He stood, as well. "Lindsey, just listen for a minute, okay? What is important here, at least to me, is that I did not willingly come to your house and crawl into your bed. I wasn't the one who created the situation."

"Neither was my father," she replied and went into the house.

He gave his head a quick shake. The woman was blind to her father's faults and there wasn't a thing he could do about it, except maybe put a little space between them for a few hours.

Jared walked back around to his truck, got in and drove away from the house.

He had no particular destination in mind. He followed various winding roads in the Hill Country, his thoughts miles away. He was surprised when he eventually recognized that he was on the outskirts of San Antonio.

By then, he realized that he needed to eat. He pulled into the first restaurant he saw.

While he ate, he thought about Lindsey. About their week together. About how happy he'd been with her. He had a hunch that maybe he was more emotionally involved with her than he'd intended. His chest hurt, for some reason. What difference did any of this make now? Christmas was next week. Another week and they'd leave here, and that would be it.

Nothing had happened to change their original plans. If Lindsey wanted to believe her father was a saint, who was he to attempt to ruin her illusions? At least the mystery was solved for him, which was important.

He hoped they could part as good friends.

It was dark when he pulled into the driveway and there were no lights on in the house. Not a good sign, Lindsey sitting there in the dark. He hadn't helped the situation any by leaving without telling her.

He supposed it wouldn't hurt to work on their communication skills—outside of bed, that is, since that was one place where they seemed to have no trouble letting their wants and needs be known to each other.

He walked into the house and flipped on the light switch.

"Lindsey?" he called, walking into the hall.

She didn't answer. He walked into the bedroom and turned on the light. The bed had been made up and the room straightened, but there was no sign of her.

He went into the kitchen and flipped on the light. A piece of paper taped to the coffeemaker caught his attention.

He pulled the paper off the coffeemaker and opened it.

J,

A friend is giving me a ride to the airport. I've decided to go to New York a little early. I would appreciate your keeping my belongings until I can have them sent to me. I placed what I couldn't take in the storage area off your back porch. L

So this was the way she wanted to play it, was it? He supposed it was as good as any. He almost felt relieved that he didn't have to make awkward conversation with her.

Why did he feel depressed just because she decided to leave early? He looked at the note again. He supposed it was because he'd hoped that they could continue as friends.

There was no hope for that now.

Eleven

"You're in love with her, you know."

Jared stared at his mother in disgust. "You know better than that."

"Do I? Well, let's look at this. She's been gone now for—what?—almost two weeks. You've been going around looking like you lost your best friend ever since. You refused to celebrate Christmas with us. You're leaving early to go overseas. I think you miss her because you're in love with her."

"Dream on."

"Of course I wouldn't have bought all of those deliciously sexy clothes for her to wear if you'd bothered to tell me the truth." She paused and tilted her head slightly. "By the way, did they work?"

"I can't believe you'd ask me such a question!"

She nodded. "They worked, or your ears wouldn't be turning red."

"You know, Gail," Joe drawled from across the table, "it's none of your business what he did on his honeymoon."

She laughed. "I know! But I do love to see my sophisticated world-traveling son blushing. I never thought I'd live to see the day."

"If you're through having fun at my expense, I think I'll go home now. I apologize about Christmas, but I wasn't in a celebrating mood. What I really wanted was silence, which is what I had."

"Don't worry about it," Joe said, standing at the same time Jared did. "We missed you, of course, but the others didn't make it home, either. You've got your own lives and we understand that. I hate to see you so down, though."

"Did I tell you I decided not to discuss the matter with the senator? I figured he'd lie about it, anyway. I'm moving on."

Jared drove up to his house and turned off the truck engine. He sat there staring at the place in which he'd been staying. Everything was back to normal. Lindsey's belongings were gone so there was no trace of her.

He wished they hadn't made love the night they got home. As soon as he crawled into bed each night, memories of that night washed over him. He'd stripped the bed and put on fresh sheets, but her essence continued to linger in the room.

His dreams disturbed him. They were a mix of his time with her in Cancun and some kind of fantasies his subconscious kept dreaming up to annoy him. Whether he was asleep or awake, his mind was on Lindsey.

But he was not in love with her.

He didn't want to be married, either to her or to anyone.

He liked his life exactly the way it was, which was why

he continued to sit in his truck and look at the house with no lights on.

Irritated with himself, Jared got out of the truck and went inside. He'd thought about going into town and shooting some pool, but the idea of walking into the Mustang didn't appeal to him.

He thought about calling one of the women he'd been seeing, but since he *was* married, he wasn't comfortable with the idea.

Some marriage. It had lasted for eight days. And nights. He should be thankful everything happened the way it did. Had she stayed, they'd be playing house, pretending that they were in a real marriage—a marriage in which they talked about having children, and him quitting his job someday so he wouldn't spend so much of his time overseas.

Funny how he could visualize Lindsey so clearly, holding a baby to her beautiful breasts, or dealing with a two-year-old or someone Heather's age.

He'd never before given a thought to having a family, to settling down, so why was it he couldn't seem to get rid of those thoughts now?

He was bored. Maybe he'd go to Houston and hang out with some of his geologist buddies there until it was time to return overseas. Good idea.

A very good idea.

Janeen White, a fun-loving redhead, was worried about Lindsey. She'd been much too quiet ever since she'd arrived two weeks ago. Janeen had never seen her unflappable friend so despondent.

Lindsey spent most of her time in bed. She slept the days away as though the world was too much for her to face. She made no effort to get dressed or comb her hair, unless Janeen nagged, or eat, unless Janeen stuck a plate in front of her and demanded she eat what was on it. Even then she only picked at her food, rearranging it more than eating it.

Janeen wasn't too clear about what had happened. All she knew was that Lindsey insisted everything was fine. Cancun was fine. The water was fine. The hotel was fine. Her stay there was fine.

Everything was just fine, except Lindsey was obviously miserable. She refused to discuss Jared, which meant that whatever had happened, her relationship with Jared was far from fine and Lindsey was taking it hard.

Today Janeen was determined to do something about it.

She opened Lindsey's door without knocking and said, "Happy New Year's Eve morning, Lindsey. Here, I brought you a cup of coffee to help you get started celebrating."

Lindsey stood at the bedroom window with her arms crossed, still in her pajamas, staring out at the falling snow. "Thank you, Janeen. That's kind of you." She didn't turn around. "Please set it on the dresser."

Ignoring her, Janeen placed the cup in Lindsey's hand before she stretched out on the nearby lounge. "You know, you've been here for two weeks and have barely said more than two words at a time. We talked more during our weekly phone conversations than we have since you arrived."

Lindsey held the cup with both hands, as though to warm them. Her lips turned up at each corner in a travesty of a smile. "Sorry. I know I haven't been very good company. I've just had a lot on my mind."

"I'm a little confused about what happened once you got back from Cancun. Would you run that past me again?"

Janeen was counting on Lindsay's innate politeness to keep her from kicking her out the room. She watched Lindsey struggle with her very real desire to say, "It's none of your business. Leave me alone."

So she waited, looking out the window as though she, too, were fascinated by the big snowflakes floating past. Eventually, Lindsey walked over to the bed and sat down against the headboard. She held one of her pillows against her chest as if it offered emotional protection. She sighed.

"You were right, Janeen. I should have never gotten married."

"Ah." Janeen studied her friend closely. "Boy, he must have been a real dud in bed, huh?"

Lindsey gave an unladylike snort. "On the contrary. He was the answer to every woman's dreams."

Janeen looked at her with raised brows. "That good, huh?"

Silence stretched out.

Lindsey gave a heartfelt sigh. "Nooo…that wasn't the problem."

Janeen's eyes twinkled. "That's good. Whooeee," she said, flicking her fingers as though they were burning, "then he must have been boorrring out of bed. What a letdown. Too bad we can't seem to find guys who're fun to be with *and* great in bed. Guess we can't have everything."

Lindsey stared into space as though her mind were somewhere else.

Janeen waited. She might be irritating Lindsey with her comments but at least she was pulling her out of the numb state that had so worried Janeen.

"Jared is very entertaining," Lindsey eventually said, sounding thoughtful. "He's warm and tender, loves to tease, doesn't take himself too seriously, makes me feel beautiful, treats me like I'm someone very special to him."

Janeen studied Lindsey in silence, watching her expression change from blank to pain. She loved Lindsey and she hated to think that anyone had hurt her so badly.

In a musing tone, Janeen said, “Well, no wonder you couldn’t put up with him for a more than a week. Sounds like a louse, through and through.”

Lindsey choked and started laughing. Janeen grinned at her friend until she realized that Lindsey’s laughter had turned into tears.

Janeen rushed over to the bed and wrapped her arms around her friend. “Tell me,” she whispered, holding her close. “You’re safe here with me, Lindsey.”

“I know,” she said, wiping her eyes. “The truth is, I somehow managed to screw up my life because, once again, I believed in my father.”

“And now you don’t?”

Lindsey shook her head. “Did I tell you that I called him Christmas Day? He’s very upset that I’ve moved here and was giving me one of his lectures, when I stopped him by telling him of the absurd story the Crenshaws had cooked up about him.”

“What kind of absurd story?”

“That my dad was the person behind Jared being in my bed.”

Janeen stared at her, practically speechless. Finally, she said, “No kidding?”

“No kidding, but I told Jared and his father that it was a pack of lies to smear my father.”

“Only it wasn’t a lie.”

More tears fell. “When I told Dad what I’d heard, he got all pompous and in his father-knows-best voice told me that he’d only done it for my own good. That the Crenshaws are a powerful family in the state. That he knew I’d be well taken care of. That the connection would be of mutual benefit to them as well as to him. That after all his planning to get me married, I had the nerve to run off to New York, anyway, despite his wishes."

"Why, that old buzzard! What a sleazebucket."

As though a dam had suddenly burst inside her, Lindsey poured out her hurt between sobs.

"Janeen…my whole life…has been a lie…everything I've believed about my dad…has been a lie…I thought I had…good judgment…about people…and I don't…oh, Janeen, I don't…and it h-hurts…so much…my dad…is nothing…like I thought…he's a h-horrible man…he uses people…he doesn't care…who it is…not even me… I…I'm nothing more…to him…than…than…a commodity…to use to…get something…he wants…oh Janeen…it h-hurts so much…what am I…going…to do? I'll never…be able to…face Jared again…after all the things…I said about him…and his f-father."

Janeen was normally not a violent person, but if the good senator had been there at that moment, she would have shot him and considered it justifiable homicide!

She murmured soothing, nonsensical phrases while she held on to her friend, letting Lindsey purge herself of some of the heartache she was feeling.

When Lindsey's bout of tears subsided, Janeen slipped away and went into the bathroom. She wet a washcloth with cool water, wrung out the excess and took it to Lindsey. "Here, sweetie, put this against your eyes. I'm going to make us some tea. Coffee is good for what ails you, but tea is definitely a comfort drink."

When Janeen returned, Lindsey was in the bathroom. Janeen could hear the water running—Lindsey was in the shower. She waited and eventually Lindsey opened the door, wearing her fleecy bathrobe and a towel around her head.

Lindsey's eyes looked awful, so swollen, Janeen knew it must be painful for her to keep them open.

"Thank you," Lindsey said hoarsely, accepting the cup of tea. "For much more than the tea. Thank you for being my friend, for understanding me so well."

"That's what friends are for," Janeen replied.

They returned to their previous positions and sipped on their tea in companionable silence. Time passed. Janeen didn't care. There was nothing more important for her to do today than be there for her friend.

"You know," Lindsey said, "one of the really awful things, one of the most humiliating things that happened, is that Jared asked me to marry him even though he didn't want to get married."

"Why would he do that, do you suppose?"

Lindsey's lips quivered and she bit down hard on her bottom lip. "Because he wanted to do the right thing and my dad was throwing such a fit."

"Really! What was in it for Jared, do you suppose?"

"What do you mean?"

"Well, I can't believe the man's so altruistic that he'd marry you out of the kindness of his heart. I mean, come on. He must have gotten some benefit out of marrying you. What do you think that was?"

Lindsey gave her a suspicious look. When Janeen continued to look at her without smiling, she said, "He kept me in bed with him for a week. I suppose that was a benefit of sorts."

"True," Janeen replied thoughtfully. "What else?"

"Oh, I don't know," Lindsey replied peevishly, "to make my dad happy, okay?"

"But I thought you told me that he didn't need your dad's influence or support," Janeen replied.

"He doesn't."

"So, what's the deal here?"

"There was such a change in him! I mean, once I walked out on him at a local café, we never spoke again. Not until Thanksgiving when my dad had his heart attack—probably his fake heart attack, for all I know—but it worked, didn't it? I contacted Jared and practically begged him to marry me."

"And that's when he should have told you to get lost and leave him alone."

A tear slipped down Lindsey's cheek. "I know. Instead, he immediately agreed that we should get married as soon as possible."

"Oh, sweetie, I think that poor husband of yours did everything in his power to right a wrong he wasn't responsible for in the first place."

"Of course he did! Don't you see? I ruined any chance we might have had to make the marriage work!"

Janeen raised her eyebrows. "Really. So…you want the marriage to continue."

"Obviously not now. I never want to face the man again."

"Are you saying that you're in love with him?"

"That's the absolute worst thing that could have happened under the circumstances, and yes, that's exactly what I'm telling you."

"Oh, Lindsey, I'm so terribly sorry."

"You warned me. You told me to stop caving in to my dad's demands."

"Yes, but if you love Jared, then marrying him was the right thing to do."

"For all the wrong reasons." Lindsey got off the bed and

rewet the washcloth, then returned to the bed and covered her eyes again.

"Doesn't matter, you know. The fact is that you fell in love with your own husband. How neat is that? So are you going to let your father's behavior stop you from being with the man you love?"

"He hates me, Janeen." She lifted the cloth and looked at her friend. "In fact, Jared thinks I was part of Dad's machinations."

"So tell him you weren't. Tell him you want to start all over. Call him."

"I can't."

"You're being a coward."

"Right the first time."

"What if he's in love with you?"

"Don't make me laugh."

"Actually, I'd very much like to make you laugh—I haven't heard you laugh since you arrived. From everything you've said, I think the week in Cancun was about more than sex. But you'll never know if you don't talk to him and explain why you left so abruptly and how you feel about everything now that you know the truth."

Lindsey got off the bed and began to pace. "He's going to Saudi Arabia in a week or so. It won't matter what I might say to him, he's leaving the country. Which is just as well." She continued to pace with jerky steps. "I wouldn't know what to say to him. 'Sorry you got involved with the Russells'? Well, I'm sure he is, too. No, it's over. I'm sticking to our plan. That's the best and most loving thing I can do for him—give him his freedom."

"Do I hear something of the martyr in your voice? 'Oh, that's all right. I'll suffer in silence, never letting him know how I feel about him. It's okay.'"

Lindsey spun around on her heel, her face flushed with anger. Janeen didn't care. She'd gotten her friend out of her funk—at least temporarily.

"You're really being obnoxious, you know that, don't you?"

"Sure do. Call him."

"All right! I'll call him! Are you satisfied?"

Janeen silently handed her the cordless phone.

Lindsey looked horrified. "Not now! Not today. I'll call him tomorrow, first thing in the morning. I'll wish him a happy new year and good luck on his job and tell him that I now know the truth about my father. I'll apologize for what I had said, then I'll hang up."

Janeen stood. She'd done all she could. The rest was up to Lindsey. "Tomorrow. Good idea. You'll be starting off the new year with a clean slate."

Lindsey nodded her head. "Yes."

Janeen walked out of the bedroom and closed the door behind her before rolling her eyes in exasperation. She knew Lindsey well enough to know that she would find logical and reasonable excuses not to call Jared until after he left the States.

However, Janeen felt that she'd given Lindsey an opportunity to think things through more clearly, at least where Jared was concerned. As far as the senator, Janeen had taken a personal delight in delivering Lindsey's message that she didn't want to talk to him when he'd called this morning. Until now, she hadn't known why and figured that Lindsey didn't want to weaken her resolve to stay in New York by speaking to him.

Her friend would heal, she knew. Too bad she would do it without giving her marriage a chance.

* * *

That evening Janeen stuck her head around Lindsey's door. "I'm leaving now. Are you sure you don't want to come with me? Tonight's the biggest party of the year. There's plenty of room for you if you'll change your mind."

Lindsey looked up from the book she was reading. "Thanks for the invitation, Janeen. I'm just not in a partying kind of mood, I'm afraid. You've helped me today by being here for me and I appreciate it more than I can say. Go. Have a blast. You can tell me all about it tomorrow."

"Well, okay," Janeen said with a sigh. She closed the door and then opened it again. "Oh! I almost forgot. I found a tall, good-looking cowboy at the front door. You won't mind if I take him with us tonight, will you? He definitely looks like my kind of guy!"

"A cowboy?" Lindsey repeated, putting her book down. "You mean here?"

"Yep. I opened the door and there he was, all bundled in a sheepskin coat, wearing boots and a western hat. You should get a look at those blue eyes! I'm going to—"

That's all Janeen got out of her mouth before her closest friend pushed around her and ran toward the living room. Janeen smiled to herself. It might turn out to be a good new year after all.

Twelve

Lindsey stopped abruptly at the end of the hallway. Why had she come racing out here like this?

Because you're thrilled he's here!

What was she going to say to him?

What you planned to tell him on the phone.

What was he doing here?

Here's an idea. Why don't you stop hovering in the hall, go into the living room and ask him?

She touched her hair. It was a mess. She needed to go back and—

You do realize that you're being ridiculous. Jared has seen your hair messed up before. In fact, he's helped to mess it up on several occasions. Go!

Lindsey walked into the living room. Jared stood just inside the door, holding his hat. When he saw her, his initial response almost undid her. The look of love and longing—along with his beautiful smile—caused her throat to close. Then his face was wiped clear of all expression and she wondered if she'd imagined that he'd appeared to be glad to see her.

She paused and stared at him, drinking in his presence, wanting him so badly she thought she might die from the ache.

"Jared. What a surprise," she said, inwardly blessing Janeen for getting her out of bed, bathed and shampooed—as well as dressed—today.

Janeen had described him well. He wore a heavy coat, that came to the knees of his jeans, and his boots. He'd never looked so good to her.

She clasped her hands tightly so that she wouldn't run across the room and throw her arms around his neck, begging for his forgiveness. Lindsey heard Janeen behind her and turned around to introduce them. For the first time she noticed how Janeen was dressed and for a moment, she was speechless. Her tall, statuesque friend had on a silver lamé gown that clung to her voluptuous curves. No way could she be wearing underwear without it showing.

"Janeen, I'd like to introduce you to Jared Crenshaw. I may have mentioned him to you."

When she looked at Lindsey Janeen's expression projected her thoughts so clearly, Lindsey was certain that Jared could easily interpret them. "I'm very pleased to meet you, Mr. Crenshaw," she said graciously. "You're Lindsey's husband, aren't you?"

"I am," he responded with no hesitation.

"Oh, darn," Janeen replied, her eyes filled with mischief. "You're already married," she said with an exaggerated pout. "Just my luck. Do they grow many good-looking guys like you down in Texas?"

He tried not to laugh, Lindsey could tell, but his grin kept escaping. "As a matter of fact, ma'am, there's a bunch of them like me, and most of them are kinfolk."

Janeen grabbed her chest. "Oh, be still, my heart. I'm moving to Texas tomorrow."

"And this," Lindsey said dryly, "is my incorrigible friend, Janeen White."

Jared held out his hand. "I'm pleased to meet you, ma'am. Lindsey speaks of you often."

Lindsey noted that Jared kept his eyes focused solely on Janeen's face, despite the shimmering dress—which won him an untold amount of spousal points.

Janeen dropped her teasing and shook his hand. "I'm so glad to finally get to meet you, Jared. Lindsey's told me a great deal about you. Sorry I left you standing there like that. I wasn't sure how Lindsey was going to—"

"Aren't you supposed to be going somewhere?" Lindsey cut in hurriedly.

Jared's impassive expression gave no hint of what he might be thinking. "I hope you don't believe everything she says about me, even if it's true."

Janeen turned and looked at Lindsey, fluttering her lashes, and Lindsey knew Janeen was capable of saying the most outrageous things. She cringed to think of all the many answers Jared might hear.

She needn't have worried. Janeen looked back at Jared, her smile heartwarming. "I've only heard good things about you, believe me."

Lindsey was disconcerted to see the look of surprise on Jared's face.

"Well, I'm out of here, guys," Janeen said. "Enjoy your evening. I doubt I'll make it home much before three." She picked up her floor-length wrap and draped it over her shoulders. "I'm glad I had the chance to put a face to the name, Jared. Take care."

After Janeen left the only sound in the room was the ticking of the wall clock. Jared looked at it and did a double take.

Lindsey smiled. "You'd have to know Janeen, Jared. She's never predictable."

The sophisticated lady who had just left them had a clock shaped like a cat, with a tail that swished back and forth at every beat and eyes that rolled in time.

"She said that Oscar was the only pet her landlord allowed her to have, so he has a prominent place in the apartment."

"Ah."

Feeling more nervous now that they were alone, Lindsey walked toward him and asked, "May I take your coat? Would you like something to drink?"

She thought he seemed to relax a little, but she could be imagining it.

He slipped out of the coat and handed it to her. "Coffee sounds good," he said, blowing on his fingers. "I should have grabbed my gloves."

Lindsey hung his coat in the hall closet and when she headed for the kitchen, Jared followed her.

She trembled so that it would be her luck to spill coffee grounds everywhere when she measured out the coffee. She glanced at him and said conversationally, "I can't get over the surprise of your being here. When did you arrive?"

He glanced at his watch. "A couple of hours ago, I guess."

"Oh! Will you be staying in New York long?"

He shrugged. "'Fraid not. I'm on my way to Saudi and decided to leave enough time in my travel schedule to drop by to see you."

She had such a thick lump in her throat, she wasn't certain she could talk. He must have gotten over some of his anger at her and her father if he was willing to look her up.

"Oh." Lindsey stepped back from the counter with a sigh of relief. The coffee was now dripping into the carafe and she hadn't spilled a thing. "Why don't we go into the living room? The coffee won't take long."

She led the way and motioned for him to sit. She chose a chair across from him. "How did you find me?"

"It wasn't difficult. Whoever answers the phone at your dad's office not only knew Janeen's last name but gave me the address, as well."

"Oh. Well." She looked at her hands clasped in her lap.

After a slight pause, they both spoke at once.

"It's quite a coincidence that you showed up here tonight. I was planning to call—"

"I didn't really figure you'd want to see me but I—"

They stopped at the same time and stared at each other. After a moment, he said, "You were going to call me?"

"Uh-huh. Yes. I was going to wish you a happy new year."

"Oh. Well, I guess you don't have to call to do that now."

There was another long pause, which enabled Lindsey to hear the gurgle of the coffeepot as it completed its task.

"Oh! The coffee's ready. I'll be right back."

By the time she returned with the coffee, Lindsey felt a little more composed. She handed him his cup and sat down again. After another rather lengthy pause, they spoke in unison.

"I wanted to apologize—"

Lindsey grinned, he grinned back, and they both began to laugh, which cleared some of the tension in the room. She waved her hand at him. "You first."

"I just wanted to apologize for going off and leaving

without telling you. I guess I wasn't thinking too clearly at the time."

"And I wanted to apologize for *my* behavior that day. You'd done nothing wrong and I was inexcusably rude. I'm so sorry that I blamed you and your father of lying about my father, when, in fact, you were telling the truth."

He looked surprised. Of course he was surprised—how many lectures had he been forced to listen to extolling her father's many virtues?

"Then you do believe your father was behind my ending up in your bed?"

"I know he was because he freely admitted it, thinking he'd done me a real service—and himself, too, of course."

"I'm afraid I'm not following you."

"I can't tell you how humiliated I am over his actions. You see, he decided—without discussing it with me, of course—that I should marry a Crenshaw, and you happened to be available. You made it easier for him by asking me out a few times, which fit perfectly with his plans. He wanted to compromise us and shame you into marrying me. Which he did."

He didn't comment right away. Instead, he studied his coffee intently as though he might find in its depths something polite to say. It was her turn to be surprised when he said, "I want to be completely honest with you, Lindsey, so there will be no misunderstanding later. That wasn't why I married you."

"It wasn't?"

"No. My initial reason was to help my family deal with your father. They've spent months trying to get a water rights bill out of the committee your father chairs. Things were finally moving forward when all of this happened. After that, your father didn't seem to have time to accept or return their phone calls."

"My father's manipulations never end, do they?"

"There's something else that I need to tell you where your father is concerned and, believe me, I'll understand if you kick me out the door when I do."

"I can't think of anything you could say about my father that would cause me to defend him."

"The Crenshaws are looking for a qualified candidate to challenge your father when the next election rolls around. Dad had the investigator he hired to find out who was behind my abduction continue to follow one of the leads he happened to come across. What he found would be enough to put your father behind bars."

Jared shook his head wearily. "I figured I owed you the truth. I can't tell you how sorry I am that you're caught in the middle, but the fact is, my family is going to go to great lengths to put him out of office."

"For good reason, it appears."

His eyes narrowed. "I figured you'd be upset when I told you."

"Believe me, upset doesn't begin to cover what I've been feeling since I spoke to my father on Christmas. That's when he admitted—actually bragged about—what he had done. Since then I've had to deal with who my father really is. I've had to look at my entire life from a new—and very depressing—perspective." She smiled at him, although now that she knew Jared's real reason for marrying her, she felt like crying.

When she first saw him there in the apartment, she'd had a wild hope that he'd come to tell her he didn't want to continue their original plan to divorce, that he wanted to stay married. *Still not ready to face reality, are you?*

Their marriage had never had a chance to work. "I appreciate your being honest about why you married me."

"I said that was my initial reason." He tugged on his earlobe, and she knew that he only did that when he was nervous. Nothing else had given her a clue to what he was thinking and feeling since he'd arrived.

"You had others?" she finally asked.

"None of them particularly admirable, but since we're being honest with each other I have to admit that."

She was intrigued by the fact that his ears were red. "Care to confess?" she asked lightly, as though his answer really didn't matter to her.

He cleared his throat. "The truth is that I wanted to make love to you since the night I met you. When everything happened, I figured that I might as well marry you because I knew that would be the only way I could get you into bed."

Her face felt hot and she knew her embarrassment was apparent. "Mission accomplished."

He nodded, looking grim. Without looking at her, he said, "Except the joke's on me."

"Oh?"

He looked down at his hands. "Yeah," he said in a low voice. "I did something really stupid. I fell in love with you." He glanced at her and then away, staring at the Christmas decorations that were still in place.

He couldn't have said that he was in love with her. She must have imagined those words coming out of his mouth. "What did you say?" she asked faintly.

"I know," he said with disgust. "Falling in love wasn't part of our agreement, but I wanted you to know. I guess I wanted you to know all the truth, as long as I was confessing everything else." He stood and said, "Look, I've got to go."

She sat staring up at him in complete and total shock. Jared loved her? Could this really be happening to her after all the pain she'd gone through?

She stood as he walked back from the hall pulling on his coat. He reached into one of the pockets and brought out a small box. "I've been in Houston for the past few days. While I was there I happened to see this and it made me think of you." He glanced down at the gift. "It's nothing, really."

Numbly, she accepted the box. He was leaving. He'd said what he came to say and he was leaving, despite telling her that he loved her! She had to stop him from leaving.

Lindsey opened the gift and found a bracelet. When she picked it up, she saw why he'd thought of her. Interspersed with delicate diamonds and rubies were tiny dolphins, dancing and leaping, with the sweetest smiles on their faces.

"Oh, Jared," she whispered brokenly.

"I hope you like it," he said, sounding diffident.

She looked him in the eye and said, "I love it, Jared Crenshaw, so very much, but not a tenth as much as I love you."

He blinked and his impassive expression changed to a look of wonder. And of hope. Cautiously, he said, "You know, just because I told you how I feel doesn't mean you have to—" She effectively cut him off by covering his mouth with hers, with what she hoped he'd recognize as all the love and passion she had inside her.

He wrapped his arms around her and took over the kiss as though he were a starving man at a banquet. By the time he lifted his head from hers, they were both breathing hard.

"When does your plane leave?" she asked.

"Tomorrow evening. I have a room at one of the hotels near the airport."

"Stay here tonight. Please."

"Are you sure?"

"I've never been more certain of anything in my entire life."

With a shout of joy, Jared picked her up and strode toward the hallway. She put her arms around his neck, kissing his chin, his cheek, his ear and along his jaw, pausing only long enough to say, "Second door on the right," before she continued.

They were out of their clothes and beneath the covers in record time. Their coming together was explosive. They held each other with fierce pleasure, never slowing down, until they fell over the edge of passion into climactic bliss.

Jared continued to hold her close. He kissed and caressed her, bringing them both to a state of arousal yet again.

Lindsey couldn't believe what had happened tonight. Jared had searched her out and now he was here in her bed—an obvious miracle that she refused to question.

This time they made love lazily, moving slowly, sharing languid touches and sweet kisses, murmuring words that only lovers can say until their movements finally quickened and they climaxed once again.

They lay quietly, her head on his shoulder. He smiled at her and said, "Tonight reminds me of some of the dreams I've been having since you left. Only much, much better because I know this is real and not some dream."

"If I'd waited until tomorrow to call, you would have already been gone."

"Do you have any idea how difficult it was for me to come see you when I had no idea what my reception might be? Then Janeen seemed to be gone forever and I thought you'd refused to see me."

"I'm going to have a little talk with my friend, Janeen. She stood there chatting with me without telling me you were here. As soon as she mentioned a good-looking cowboy in our living room, I practically knocked her down getting out the door."

"You hid your enthusiasm quite well. You were at your most regal when you greeted me—all polite manners and no way for me to tell how you felt about my being here."

She grinned. "I believe you know how I feel now, don't you?"

He frowned. "I'm not all that sure. Maybe if you could show me once again..."

She had no trouble at all convincing him by the time they finally fell asleep, toward morning.

The next morning Lindsey and Jared tiptoed into the kitchen to make coffee. Lindsey hadn't heard Janeen come home. There had been too many distractions at the time, she supposed. Regardless, she wanted to give her the chance to sleep in. Janeen had to go to work tomorrow. For that matter, so did Lindsey.

Exciting thought, but no more exciting than to have Jared here for a few more hours.

They were seated at the kitchen table drinking coffee when Jared said, "I have to admit that I'd hoped you'd be willing to listen to me when I arrived, because I wanted to ask you if you'd be willing to start over with me."

"Start what over?" she asked, puzzled by his expression.

"Our marriage."

"Oh. Well, I thought we already had. Wasn't that what last night was all about? Making new commitments to each other?"

"There's no question we're compatible in bed, sweetheart, but, generally speaking, when a couple marries they've spent enough time together to get to know each other really well. Other than a few dates and a week in Cancun together, we know very little about the other."

"I disagree. We were thrown into a crisis situation and

we managed to get through it. You've had to deal with my blind spot where my father is concerned. I've had to deal with the fact that you don't want to be married. So what's your idea of starting over? Go back to the 'Hello, I'm Jared Crenshaw' stage?"

"Of course not. We're married. I want us to continue on from here as a married couple starting on a new adventure, without the specter of your father hanging over us." He lifted her hand and pressed her knuckles against his mouth. "Besides, I may not have wanted to get married at first, but now I can't face the thought of not being married to you. I fell hook, line and sinker for you. That's not going to go away, nor do I want it to."

"Well," she said, trying to be pragmatic about their situation, "we'll have to postpone sharing our life histories until you come back, won't we? Do you know how long you'll be gone?"

"Not really, no. Hopefully no later than September, possibly October. However, I'm not dropping off the planet, you know." He smiled. "We can e-mail each other. In fact, that may be the only way I can concentrate on what you tell me. I find your presence to be more than a little distracting."

From the look in his eye, he was ready to be distracted yet again.

"I'm not looking forward to nine months without you," she said wistfully. "Two weeks was bad enough."

"Nine months? You trying to tell me something?"

She chuckled. "No. That's how long you'll be gone."

"Oh. Well, you'll tell me if there's going to be a change in our family status, won't you?"

"You'll be the first person I tell. You can count on it." Lindsey got up and poured them more coffee and when she sat down, she said, "How can you sound so accepting of the separation, Jared?"

"Easy. I've just gone through two weeks thinking I'd never see you again, much less make love to you. That I would never again fall asleep with you in my arms, or hear you laugh, or see your eyes sparkle or watch you when you get excited. Not having you in my life at all is my idea of hell. I can stand to be away from you for a few months knowing that you'll be waiting for me when I come home." He looked at his watch. "I'm going to have to leave in another hour. Do you think we could continue our conversation in the bedroom?"

"Certainly, Mr. Crenshaw. What subject shall we discuss?" she asked, following him back to the bedroom.

"Anatomy," he said, slipping her robe off and leaving her bare.

Taken aback, she said, "Why that particular subject, if I may ask?"

He scooped her up and fell into bed with her. "I've discovered how much I enjoy learning anatomy by the Braille system," he said, and proceeded to demonstrate his expertise.

Thirteen

January 15th
Hi sweetheart. Sorry I haven't written sooner. There's been a lot of changes since I was here before. Things have settled down a little so I'll be able to write more frequently. I'm sending my love with this. Tell your crazy roommate hello for me. Jared

January 15th
What a relief to hear from you. It's been a very long two weeks since you were here. I kept checking to see if Oscar the cat had stopped swishing his tail.

I love working at the museum. Being there every day has been such a joy and I'm already learning so much about the behind-the-scenes work that goes on. The security is absolutely amazing, but not surprising considering what a treasure trove of art we have here. Please take care of yourself for me. Your loving wife.

February 14th
Will you be my valentine? I bought you something to celebrate the holiday and then decided to wait until I got home to give it to you. I remember the bracelet gift and how lavishly affectionate you were. Figure it wouldn't hurt to hang on to this one for a while so I can receive your marvelous way of saying 'thanks' in person. Miss you, too. Love, J

February 14th
Hmm. Lavishly affectionate, am I? That's good to know. Of course, I may have forgotten everything you taught me by the time September rolls around, and you'll have to teach me again.

I'm still enjoying work. I really like the woman who supervises me. I'm still amazed at how busy we are. Thank you for writing every day. Hearing from you gives me such a boost. Sometimes I catch myself wondering if I'd dreamed the time we spent together. If so, I want to keep on dreaming.

Love you, Me

March 26
Glad you finally spoke to your dad again. You don't have to spend time with him if you don't want to, but he does love you in his own possessive way. I'm sure the man has some good points, even though I haven't seen them. (Trying for a little humor there.) As always, you sound as though you were polite enough.

Dad e-mailed to say they've found a highly qualified

man with integrity to run for your dad's office, and he's already getting a lot of support. Playing games with our lives is one scheme that turned around and bit him in the, uh...butt. I keep reminding myself that I benefited from his scheming. I was too stubborn to give marriage a thought until you stepped into my life. Now, I couldn't be happier.

Which leads me to a question. What are you wearing right now? I've got to figure out a way to sleep at night. Picturing you in something sexy could help—or could make things worse. Never can tell. Your homesick husband

March 26
Well, I'm sitting here in front of the computer in my frilly, frothy...naw, you'll never buy that one. We actually had snow today, can you believe it? It's almost April. So I'm in my flannel pajamas and heavy socks. That should turn you on. Besides, I'm saving all my sexy nighties for when you get back home. For some reason, they're all practically brand-new. They rode in my luggage to and from Cancun and, except for the gown I wore our first night there, were seldom (read: never) used.

It's late and I need to get to bed. I'm still learning a lot at work. With the experience I'm getting, I'm hoping to eventually qualify as a curator for a smaller museum. (Let's face it, most any one of them would be smaller!) I want to be able to be with you wherever you're sent. If there's a museum, I can always do something. If nothing else, volunteer some of my time when you have a short assignment.

Love you, love you, love you. Mrs. Jared Crenshaw

April 2
Had a sandstorm today. Not pleasant. The sand gets into

everything. I keep the computer in a sealed container and it still has sand on it when I open the box. I don't understand how anyone would want to live in a place like this, not when they could be living in God's country—Texas, that is. Missing you, J

April 2
Yes, Texas is definitely God's country. With the dust storms (Saudi Arabia doesn't have a monopoly on them, you know), droughts, floods (all in the same year), locusts, tarantulas and scorpions, Texas is straight out of the *Old Testament.*

Janeen has been dating a guy for several weeks now. I reminded her that you were going to introduce her to some Crenshaws and she told me to pass on to you that you'd better start getting them lined up in a hurry, 'cause her biological clock is making bonging sounds—forget ticking.

I had lunch with Dad today. I will never feel the same way about him, but that's probably for the best. I had him on a pedestal and now I see him without either rose-colored glasses or blinders. I certainly have no intention of being in his company more than absolutely necessary.

Oh, and you should hear his version about what's shaping up in the coming election. I sat there thinking that he's probably never told a complete truth in his entire life. Oh, excuse me. In Washington, his brand of communication is called spin. I'm so glad you aren't in politics. Love, love, love, etc. you, Lindsey

April 6
How's *your* biological clock doing, Mrs. Crenshaw? Janeen is always guaranteed to make people laugh. And

speaking of relatives, I've got a confession to make. It's not that I've been deliberately keeping this from you. I didn't think it was important until I realized how you feel about politicians these days. My Uncle Jerome is a Texas state senator and his son Jed is a U.S. representative. I understand another cousin of mine, Justin, is eyeing an elected post—land commissioner, I think.

Check with Janeen to see if she has a particular vocation she wants her husband to follow. The Crenshaws are a versatile lot. I'm sure I could find one in most any profession she can name.

Jared the matchmaker, brother to Omar the tentmaker. Well, maybe not.

Lindsey woke up in a grumpy mood. She hadn't heard from Jared in months. At least it felt that way. Today was the 12th of May and he hadn't written in two weeks, which was so unusual as to be frightening. He rarely missed a day sending her a brief note—definitely no more than two or three days.

Maybe she'd call his company's head office and see what gives. He'd tried calling her a few times but there was usually so much static and other interference that they had a difficult time understanding each other.

She walked into the kitchen and poured herself some orange juice and a cup of coffee. Janeen was already up and watching the morning news.

Lindsey had just replaced the coffee carafe on the burner when Janeen let out a wail, "Oh no, oh no, oh no-no-no, it can't be!"

She left her coffee and juice and ran into the living room. "What? What is it? What's wrong?"

Janeen sat on the sofa, her hand over her mouth and a look of horror on her face. She pointed to the television screen.

"…the suicide bomber has been identified as part of an extremist group that has been terrorizing the area for several months…"

Lindsey looked back at Janeen. "Where? Where was the bombing?"

"Riyadh."

"Oh. Oh! Riyadh! Where Jared's headquarters are!"

Janeen stared at her mutely.

"Where exactly was the bombing?" She turned back to the television in time to watch a commercial come on. "Did they say?"

"Remember a while back when suicide bombers broke through the guards at an American compound?"

"Oh, my God. Is that what happened?"

"All I caught was Americans, several killed and many wounded."

I will not panic. There are many Americans working over there. Jared said he's often working out at the oil fields. He probably wasn't in town at all.

Lindsey found the number for the corporate headquarters in Houston. She had to start over twice before she got the sequence of numbers correct.

"Hello? Yes, I need to speak to someone about the bombing in Saudi Arabia that's being broadcast on this morning's news. My husband is there with your company. Yes. His name is Jared Crenshaw. I'm trying to find out any information you may have about him. Yes, of course I'll hold."

Janeen walked into the room behind her and slowly rubbed Lindsey's back. Lindsey gave her a quick smile while she listened to canned music playing in her ear.

"Hello. Yes, this is Mrs. Jared Crenshaw. That's right. Do you know anything about—? Oh. Do you know if he happened to be in Riyadh when the—? Oh. Yes. Yes, I understand. Would you please take the numbers where I can be reached and call me when you have any news? I know. Yes. But if there's any way— Thank you." She hung up the phone and turned to her roommate. "Oh, Janeen," she whispered and put her arms around her.

"What did they say?"

She sighed wearily. "They don't have any information that has been authenticated. They don't know where Jared is, they don't know if he was in town, they know nothing."

"But they will call you when they have some solid information, right?"

She shrugged. "Who knows? I gave them this number, my cell number and the museum's number. There's nothing else I can do."

"That's the worst of it. Feeling so helpless. It's the waiting and the wondering…"

Lindsey glanced at her watch. "I've got to go or I'm going to be late for work. I'll call you if I hear anything. You do the same."

"You can count on it."

Three days and three sleepless nights later, the phone rang at three o'clock in the morning. Lindsey picked it up before the first ring finished, her heart in her throat.

"Hello!" She heard static and a hollow sounding voice. "Hello? Who is this?"

Finally, she heard the most joyous words of all. "It's Jared. Can you hear me?"

She burst into tears. Hastily wiping them away as fast as they sprang forth, she said, "Are you all right?"

She heard his voice but his words were too garbled to decipher. When she hung up a few minutes later, she saw Janeen silhouetted in the doorway. "Is he okay?"

Lindsey hiccupped, half laughing, half crying. "I don't know. All I know is that he's alive!"

"What did he say?"

"I could only pick up a word here and there. Something about the computer kaput, Frankfurt, he loved me, he'd be coming home soon."

They stared at each other uncertainly. "He didn't say whether or not he was hurt?" Janeen asked.

Lindsey shook her head. "If he did, I couldn't make any of it out."

"Aren't overseas casualties sent to Frankfurt?"

"I think so."

They were silent, thinking about the implications.

"I don't care!" Lindsey said forcefully. "I don't care if he's lost a limb or an eye or if he's going to be in a wheelchair for the rest of his life. I don't care! He's alive and that's all I care about." She fell on the bed, sobbing.

Three days later Lindsey received a call from corporate headquarters on her cell phone. "Hello? Yes, this is she. Yes? Oh. I see. Yes, thank you. I appreciate the call."

As soon as she completed the call she immediately called Janeen. As soon as she heard her voice, Lindsey said, "The company called. He's booked on a flight to the States tomorrow. They gave me his flight number and told me when he'll be landing at Newark. The secretary who called didn't know how he was or where he was coming from. Gotta go."

She did her very best to contain her sudden need to dance, scream and shout when she went back to her duties.

* * *

Janeen met her at the door that night. "You rat! You call me and rattle off all this stuff and hang up before I can ask you a thing."

Lindsey hung up her coat. "I explained to my supervisor what was going on and she told me to take as much time as I need. She's such a nice lady. But with Jared coming back months earlier than expected, I told her that she should look for a replacement. We talked for quite a while and she offered to give me a letter of recommendation whenever I needed one. I was so touched."

She grabbed Janeen and whirled her around the room. "I can't wait until he steps off that plane. Once he's on the ground tomorrow, it will take a crowbar to pry me from his side."

"Did the secretary know whether or not he'd been injured?"

"No. But if he were seriously injured, he wouldn't be coming home on a regular international flight, would he?"

Janeen threw up her hands. "Who knows?"

Lindsey was at the airport two hours before the flight's estimated arrival time. Rather than sit around, she kept asking until she finally found someone with some authority.

"My husband's coming in from Frankfurt. He may be injured. I want to be at the gate when he comes off the plane."

"I'm sorry. Unticketed passengers are not allowed past the security gate."

"I know that. That's why I'm talking to you. Will you please give me some ID, anything that's necessary, so that I won't be arrested when I meet him at the gate?"

"No, I can't. If I make an exception for you, then everyone would expect the same treatment."

She looked at the man behind the desk—going bald, wearing glasses and looking at her with righteous determination.

He wasn't going to let her meet Jared. What if she missed him when he came through? He didn't know she would be there. He wouldn't be looking for her and she could so easily miss him.

She heard herself say, "I see. No exceptions."

"That's correct." What a supercilious jerk.

She smiled. "Fine. Then I'll go buy a ticket for whatever plane is taking off in that area." She stood and walked to the door.

"But, Mrs. Crenshaw, those are international flights."

She turned and gave him a level stare. "I'm aware of that, sir." She opened the door.

"You'd spend that kind of money just to be at the gate when your husband arrives?"

"I'll spend every penny I have if necessary." She closed the door behind her.

Next, she looked at the various international flights coming in and going out. She had a choice to fly to Rome or London. Hmm. She hadn't been to Italy in a few years—that sounded good.

Lindsey found the appropriate counter and stood in line. She had no trouble getting a ticket until she told them she had no luggage. In less than a minute she was surrounded by federal officers and taken to some kind of interrogation room.

Good thing she'd gotten to the airport early.

"What do you mean you don't intend to use the ticket? Who will?"

She sighed. "No one. All I want to do is to be able to meet my husband's flight at the gate."

"Before he clears customs?"

"Yes. Look, here's my purse. There's nothing in there that I would slip to him before he clears customs."

The gray-headed guard said, "Of course not. It's what he may give you that we're concerned about."

She smiled. "I can guarantee that all he'll be giving me is a, hopefully, passionate kiss. We were only married three weeks before he left. He's been gone for several months. He may have been injured in a suicide bombing that took place a week ago in Riyadh, Saudi Arabia. He isn't aware that I'm here and I'm afraid I won't see him with all the people coming out of customs."

The three men talked among themselves. Now she was really getting nervous because she didn't have much more time before his flight arrived.

Finally, one of them said, "Here's what we can do, ma'am. No need to buy a ticket. I'll escort you to the gate so that you can see him. After that, you and I will wait for him to clear customs. That's the best we can do."

"Oh, yes! Thank you so much." She looked at her watch. "We need to leave now if we're going to make it."

The next thing she knew, Lindsey was whisked through several Employees Only doors and came out onto the international concourse.

She'd made it.

The upside to being in a restricted area was the lack of a crowd. There were a few passengers waiting to board flights, some airport and airline employees, but she had a clear view of the gate and passageway where Jared would appear.

The only downside—and it was a very big one—came when the plane arrived. The passengers trickled out and none of them were Jared.

Don't panic. It's a big plane. Lots of people on it. He's on the plane. He's got to be on the plane.

Two flight attendants came out and her heart sank. Flight attendants didn't leave until the plane was empty, did they?

She began to walk toward them to ask if there were any other passengers when she saw him, slowly coming down the ramp. He must have lost at least thirty pounds since January. He looked much too pale and he was drawn and obviously exhausted.

He was the most beautiful sight she'd ever seen.

Jared didn't see her until he was close enough for her to say, "Welcome home, cowboy." He stopped and stared at her as if he were seeing a ghost. He blinked a couple of times, rubbed both hands over his face and walked toward her, his wonderful smile turned on at full wattage.

She met him halfway with her arms open wide.

Epilogue

It was June. The Crenshaws were having a party. The celebration was for Jared and it seemed that everyone in a hundred-mile radius had come to welcome him home.

He and Lindsey would be living in Houston now, not much more than a four-hour drive to the ranch. Now that he was married, Jared no longer wanted to travel and had been reassigned to the Houston office.

He stood with his arm around Lindsey's waist and greeted new arrivals. After almost an hour of shaking hands and accepting best wishes from friends and family, Jared looked too pale for Lindsey's comfort.

"I can feel you trembling," she murmured once they were alone. "Let's sit down, okay?"

He nodded. "I feel like some kind of invalid, I'm so weak."

They walked over to one of the tables that had been set up. Once seated, she said, "You've been home a few weeks.

I could still wring your neck for never letting on you were so ill."

"It comes with the territory, sweetheart. And I survived."

"But you could have told me."

"Why? What would you have done with the information?"

She smiled. "Demanded that you be sent home immediately so I could nurse you back to health."

He laughed. "And you would have done it, too."

"At least you were nowhere near the bombing. Hearing about that sent me over the edge. I really lost it."

"I'd been trying to call you right after it happened, but couldn't get through. I was on my way to Frankfurt when I managed to reach you."

"Where they promptly put you in the hospital."

"For tests, that's all."

Jake and Ashley—a very pregnant Ashley—sat down across the table from them.

Jake said. "What are you two quarreling about now?"

Jared grinned. "We're not quarreling. We're merely sharing our opinions with each other."

"Uh-huh."

"Ashley," Lindsey said, "you must be so uncomfortable these days."

Jake rubbed his wife's back. "She won't admit it, though. I've been doing whatever I can think of to ease the strain on her."

Ashley leaned her head against Jake's shoulder. "He has. He massages my back, feet and ankles every night." Her eyes sparkled as she added, "And he painted my toenails for me last night."

Jared burst into laughter as Jake said, "You could have talked all night without bringing that up."

"I think it's sweet," Lindsey said.

"That describes Jake, all right," Jared said. "Sweet."

"Cut it out," Jake growled. "Let's wait and see how you handle your pregnant wife complaining that she can't see her feet and she has to paint her nails." He shook his head. "I don't know what it is about you women and your nail polish."

Ashley winked at Lindsey. "I feel undressed without it on my toes." She held out her hands that wore no nail polish. "Of course, I gave up doing anything with these years ago. It's a waste of time for a veterinarian."

"Do you have a due date?" Lindsey asked.

"I'm supposedly due in another two weeks. But as uncomfortable as I've been these past few days, I think I might not go that long."

Jake and Jared stared at each other in dismay. Jake said, "Don't you dare have this baby here tonight."

Both women laughed.

Jared looked around and said, "Have you noticed Jude tonight, Jake? He's been remote and quieter than usual." He nodded toward Jude, who stood talking with their father. "How's his assignment in San Antonio going? Have you heard?"

"Nope," Jake replied. "Not a word. He must consider your returning in one piece worth coming home for. He's been in San Antonio now for over a year and this is the first time since our wedding that he's been here."

"Any news on Jason?"

"Same thing. Mom gets e-mails once in a while, but he never tells her where he is."

Lindsey said, "Are your brothers surprised that you've both gotten married?"

Jared and Jake looked at each other. "You could say that," Jared replied. "I believe their words were 'Better you than me,'" Jared added.

The women burst out laughing. "Famous last words," Lindsey said.

* * * * *

We hope you enjoyed
CAUGHT IN THE CROSSFIRE,
the second book in
Annette Broadrick's new Desire series,
THE CRENSHAWS OF TEXAS.
Please look for the stories of the other
Crenshaw brothers in 2005.

COMING NEXT MONTH

#1615 TERMS OF SURRENDER—Shirley Rogers
Dynasties: The Danforths
When Victoria Danforth and rebellious David Taylor were forced into close quarters on the Taylor plantation, former feuds turned into fiery passion. But unbeknownst to all, Victoria was no farmhand—she was the long-lost Danforth heiress! Could such a discovery put an end to their plantation paradise?

#1616 SINS OF A TANNER—Peggy Moreland
The Tanners of Texas
Melissa Jacobs dreaded asking her ex-lover Whit Taylor for help, but when the smashingly sexy rancher came to her aid, hours spent at her home turned into hours of intimacy. Yet Melissa was hiding a *sinful* secret that could either tear them apart, or bring them together forever.

#1617 FOR SERVICES RENDERED—Anne Marie Winston
Mantalk
When former U.S. Navy SEAL Sam Deering started his own personal protection company, the beautiful Delilah Smith was his first hire. Business relations turned private when Sam offered to change her virgin status. Could the services he rendered turn into more than just a short-term deal?

#1618 SHEIKH'S CASTAWAY—Alexandra Sellers
Sons of the Desert
Princess Noor Ashkani called off her wedding with Sheikh Bari al Khalid when she discovered that his marriage motives did not include the hot passion she so desired. Then a plane crash landed them in the center of an island paradise, turning his faux proposal into unbridled yearning…but would their castaway conditions lead to everlasting love?

#1619 BETWEEN STRANGERS—Linda Conrad
Lance White-Eagle was on his way to propose to another woman when he came across Marcy Griffin stranded on the side of the road. Circumstances forced them together during a horrible blizzard, and white-hot attraction kept their temperatures high. Could what began as an encounter between strangers turn into something so much more?

#1620 PRINCIPLES AND PLEASURES—Margaret Allison
CEO Meredith Cartwright had to keep playboy Josh Adams away from her soon-to-be-married sister. And what better way to do so than to throw herself directly into his path…and his bed. But Josh had an agenda of his own—and a deep desire to teach Meredith a lesson in principles…and pleasures!

SDCNM1004